♡RENT BOY♡

A NOVEL

VIXEN

Library and Archives Canada

ISBN 978-1-7381109-0-2 (softcover)
ISBN 9798862133530 (hardcover)

Cover design: Erethereal
Images: (Main character) Midjourney; (Hearts) Vecteezy

Printed in China

@its.vix.hun   www.erethereal.com   @erethereal_tarot

To all of the outcasts,
who dare to flip off societal norms,
every. single. day.

And to the memory of us, Hun,
and what could have been.

PROLOGUE.

The name 'Vixen' wasn't given to me at birth. No, it was bestowed upon me by the neon-lit streets and shadowed alleyways that whispered tales of passion and pain in the dark corners of the city. It's a name synonymous with allure and secrets, where raw desires intertwine with fragile hopes.

The flicker of neon lights, the scent of cheap perfume and cheaper booze, the cacophony of laughter and tears —they are the undercurrents that ripple through the world of escorting. My world. One where the margins between love and betrayal are as thin as a razor's edge, and every face wears a mask stitched together by secrets and lies.

In this life of tangled sheets and broken dreams, I've been a puppet on strings—held up by desires, manipulated by fates, pulled in all directions by forces both seen and unseen. I dance on a stage where the spotlight casts shadows so dark, they swallow me whole at times.

But amidst the mayhem and the cacophony, there's always been a faint whisper, an elusive sense of another world waiting on the other side of the looking glass. A place where choices are mine to make, where the strings that tug and bind finally unravel, leaving me… free.

In this story, you will find chaos and serenity, betrayal and redemption, darkness and—perhaps—a glimmer of light. It's a dance between dichotomies, a tumble down a rabbit hole where up is down, and the end is just another name for the beginning.

You might think you know what this story is about, considering its origins in the elusive world of escorting. Maybe you're anticipating a salacious tale brimming with lust, or perhaps a cautionary account of fallen souls and broken dreams. But while those elements may touch the pages of this narrative, it's truly a story of love. Not the kind found in fairy tales, but the raw, burning, and sometimes agonizing love that life thrusts upon us.

This isn't a work of pure fiction, nor is it an unabridged memoir. It's a reflection—a blend of my truths, the whispers of countless others, and the necessary embellishments that stories often demand. Through these pages, you will experience the dazzling highs and the despairing lows of a world few truly understand.

As you turn each page, remember that beneath the makeup, behind the glitz and the facade, pulses a heart—one that's been shattered and mended more times than I'd care to admit. This heart has known true love, and it's this very love that's driven me to share my story.

I am Vixen.

And this is my tale—one of love, loss, and redemption. Embrace it, for every word etched on these pages is a testament to the power of the human spirit, to the depths we go to find love, and the lengths we'll travel to protect it.

So, take this journey with me. From the dizzying heights of stripper poles to the plummeting lows of a fractured existence, let's fall together.

After all, every story needs an audience. And every fall, a landing—or the endless freedom of the void.

Welcome to the World of Night. Are you ready to let go?

♡ FUCKING SUNLIGHT. ♡

"Playing house? Not part of the gig"

Fucking sunlight.

My arch-nemesis, a cosmic joke on par with unsolicited dick pics and decaf coffee. It clawed at my retinas, transformed my skin into a topographical map of last night's indulgences. And not to mention the photographic harshness that came with it, turning me into the decaying corpse of a Victorian child. But today, the universe was in a forgiving mood.

The sunbeam pierced through nicotine-yellow curtains, illuminating the shimmering heart-shaped nipple covers that clung to my chest like lustful cherubs.

Ah, the effervescent glow of sequins like the winking eye of a flirtatious devil. They were my heraldic shields in the jousting arena of nightly escapades. My spangled beacons amidst a sea of tacky lingerie and fragmented tarot cards that I had apparently left scattered about. There was an art to being that fabulously trashy. And let me tell you—no one did it better.

Serving as intimate whispers of my nocturnal exploits, these nipple covers commanded attention. They commanded the night, the masquerade that was my existence. And, they commanded me. Maestro of my show. Me, the star. The little plaything in every narcissist's fantasy. But hey…

The show, Hun, must always go on.

The apartment was a shrine to straight man disarray —a series of contradictions with just the right amount of chaos: empty vodka bottles, discarded clothes ranging from the tasteful to the utterly disgraceful, and, oddly enough, a vintage Joan Jett poster hung next to an ironic print of the Mona Lisa, her inscrutable smile vandalized by a drawn-on moustache. The furniture had seen better days, but that was part of its charm… I guess.

Across the room, Greg—hunk of meat, zero seasoning —sprawled like a discarded Barbie doll. Naked, senseless, but generous—eight hundred bucks for an overnight gig was the least he could do.

I stood at the edge of the bed, a vixen in the midst of the ruins, slipping into a red thong so extravagant, it could declare its own independence, up my long, lean legs, the fabric strained against the powerful musculature beneath. My physique was one of contradiction—lithe yet powerful, graceful yet raw, a sinewy canvas of both discipline and indulgence. As the thong settled on my hips, the cool air kissed a swath of ink, a testament to both pain and artistry. There, slithering from my ribcage and trailing sensually down my thigh was an intricately designed snake tattoo. Its scales shimmered with iridescence, eyes cold and unyielding, capturing both danger and allure.

And then came the pièce de resistance, my signature cloak—I threw on a scarlet fur coat, a fiery halo of wanton extravagance. Its vibrant hue was reminiscent of rubies gleaming under the moonlight, deep and sultry with every shade of red imaginable dancing within its fibres.

But this coat wasn't just about aesthetics—it was an embodiment of my essence.

Zipping into leather pants that were morally obligated to be tight, I rounded up my tarot cards. My fingers paused, tantalized by a promising wad of twenties splayed on the dresser like a fan of temptation.

Catching my reflection in the mirror, my eyes, framed by smoky layers of dark eyeshadow, reflected the afterthought—or the aftermath—of a raucous night. My mullet, unkempt and tousled, straddled the line between rebellion and retro chic.

I was the lovechild of Harley Quinn and Damiano of Måneskin, blessed with Scorpio's forked tongue and double-edged wit. A feral mix of chaos and charm.

For the gals who know. You know?

I smirked and took out my lipstick, scrawling a sultry **Thanks, Hun!** onto the mirror, punctuating it with a lipstick kiss as ostentatious as my personality.

I snatched the cash, ready to make my exit when something else caught my eye.

A lamp—the gaudiest Tiffany lamp I had ever seen. It was so hideous, it was beautiful. It was the interior decor version of a car crash you can't look away from. I snatched it up as if rescuing a distressed damsel, then snapped my thong straps into place with a satisfied yank.

As I sauntered out, sunlight greeted me like the applause of invisible angels. For a fleeting moment, I found myself hoping—in another life, in another world—maybe I'd get to bask in that damn sunlight without the armour of irony. But for now? My kingdom of sequins, chaos, and tarnished halos awaited.

Exit stage left. The curtain falls. Another day, another slay.

As yassified as ever.

The morning was alive and teeming with the dewy mistresses of the night, their outfits telling tales of their wild ventures. A carnival of half-clad spectres and mascara streaks, as if the night had regurgitated its dark glamour onto the streets. Amidst the sultry whispers and broken stilettos, I navigated my path. The lamp, this odd relic of some illicit rendezvous, was my only companion —well, that and the phone buzzing in my pocket like an impatient lover.

The screen flashed: an image of a tarot card bearing a demon, its horns twisted into an almost sarcastic grin. Caller ID: **The Devil**.

I snorted, a cynical laugh suppressed, as I slipped the phone back into my leather pants. Just then, Roxy, some back alley escort with little to no decorum or tact, in my opinion, materialized. Leaning against a lamppost with the grace of a broken marionette. Her mascara was running a marathon down her cheeks. The poster child for the morning after pill.

"Rough night, Roxy?" I tossed the words at her like confetti as I passed, my lamp cutting through the morning fog like a beacon of bad choices.

"Fuck off, Vixen," she retorted, battling her urge to throw up. "Where's my fifty from Jack's—"

"Patience, Hun," I interjected, my words laced with a venomous sweetness. "I'll have it by the end of the week."

I pivoted, leaving Roxy to battle her nausea alone as I headed towards a grungy apartment complex, and that's when I saw them, the most grotesque of abominations to ever grace my presence—a couple. Their fingers laced together in some form of sickeningly sweet and effortless intimacy.

"I had a really great night," the scruffy-haired guy confessed, his words tinged with the soft hue of vulnerability.

For a fleeting moment, my steps lost their rhythmic confidence, revealing a tiny crack in my armour. The girl's laugh floated back, a bubble of something genuine and pure in this polluted air. The taste of their normality felt like a bitter pill.

"Me too. Wanna do this again," she murmured, her voice softly piercing the mist around me, as I rolled my eyes.

I pulled my scarlet fur coat tighter around me, as if its soft embrace could shield me from the seeping chill of unspoken desires.

With a renewed air of defiance, I strutted into my dilapidated building, my lamp still clutched like a trophy of the life I had chosen—or perhaps, that had chosen me.

I'm a busy gal—playing house? Not part of the gig.

My loft was pure organized chaos—a cosmic collision between gritty industrial brick walls and vintage decor.

The ceiling was a sprawling expanse of exposed pipes, dripping occasionally, weaving a twisted metal tapestry against the bare concrete above. But there were silver linings, quite literally, in the form of strings of Edison bulbs hung strategically around the place. They twinkled like distant stars against the night sky, turning a potentially grim setting into a whimsical wonderland.

To one side, a kitchenette sat, overtly compact and severely underused, with its dinky red fridge plastered with kitschy magnets from all over the world—a testament to the many admirers who'd passed through, each leaving behind a piece of their world.

Scattered around were a medley of mismatched cushions and throws on an old leather couch, telling tales of many a wild night and lazy mornings. The coffee table, a repurposed antique trunk, bore remnants of last night's makeup and a half-drunk bottle of Prosecco.

Yet the loft's most distinctive feature was a gleaming stripper pole that could double as Excalibur, right in front of my window.

Peeking through it—screwed to the outside wall—a neon sign in the shape of a heart belonging to the bar below, with the word '**LOVE**' written in the middle, oozed its sultry red light across every square inch of my space. She was bright.

My loft was reflective of a soul that had weathered much, celebrated even more, and was unapologetically authentic. A hoe pad with just a touch of class.

Flinging my tarot deck onto an antique bar cart that I was pretty sure was haunted, I threw myself onto my bed, a scandal of tangled sheets and restless dreams. I rummaged through a pack of StarChews, those fruity candies popular in the 90s, with the fervour of a raccoon on a midnight raid. My fingers emerged, betraying me with a yellow one.

Who the fuck likes the yellow ones?

I contorted my face as if I'd bitten into a lemon soaked in disappointment.

As I warred with my citrus enemy, my phone vibrated, buzzing like an incessant mosquito.

INCOMING CALL FROM THE DEVIL

I rolled my eyes so hard I could've seen my own brain, and let it go to voicemail. Screw it, I had more pressing matters—like the self-destructive ballet of PrideMate.

Ah, the gay dating app everyone loved to hate and hated to love. Sure, it's purpose was to find love… but I used it to sell it.

I updated my headline—**Vixen4Generous$$**—in fonts that practically screamed "disaster in Gucci boots."

Stowing my fresh wad of dollar bills into the hollowed-out corpse of a disco ball seemed not just appropriate but almost poetic. It was my treasure trove, a disco Pandora's box, half vice, half virtue.

Just as I was about to dive deeper into my financial fantasies, a jarring text notification sounded off like a fire alarm. It was from Bambi, that platinum thread in the mess of my life.

(Bambi): **Where the HELL are you?!**

The text might as well have been a slap. My eyes flared open, adrenaline surging through me like a tidal wave of regret and missed appointments. I smacked my forehead, cursing the God of Forgotten Plans.

"Fuck," I hissed, the lingering taste of yellow StarChew now a corrosive acid.

Fumbling like a manic street magician,

(Me): **Sorry! OMW!!**

Ping!

Another notification, this time from PrideMate.

(XXLPigFeet23): **Hey! How much for an hour?**

I groaned, shoving the phone into my bag like a piece of evidence I couldn't deal with right now. No time for hustles and heartbeats.

Ping!

XXLPigFeet23 was insistent.

With a grunt of frustration, and a whirlwind of fur and leather, I exited my loft, leaving behind the sultry red glow, the unanswered messages, and the yellow StarChews, lying there like a crime scene in a murder mystery only I understood.

The neon heart flickered for a moment, as if winking at me. I was its chaos. It was my ironic constancy. And out into the carnival of life I plunged, once again.

♡ BALL´S EYE. ♡

"Poor fucking baby can't handle a little orange?"

Picture a hallway with aspirations for grandeur but a budget for mediocrity. That's what I walked through—the skyscraper's corridor that tried to emulate a royal ballroom, its steel-blue walls failing miserably to hide its identity crisis. And the triangular sconces? They were casting shadows that resembled poorly drawn pentagrams. It was the aesthetic equivalent of a midlife crisis in the guise of avant-garde art.

Panting and hyper-aware of the makeup kit's sudden gravitational pull, I pounded my fist on a door like a drum solo in a death metal band. Just when I was about to give it another go—

"It's about goddamn time, Bitch." The voice was an unholy cocktail of helium and scorn.

Bambi. He was a pastel-coloured paradox, an edgy nursery rhyme underscored with trap beats. In his pink crop-top hoodie, complete with those twee light-up cat-ear headphones, he stood there like a beauty influencer who'd been hit by a kawaii truck. The epitome of a bleached bimbo twink, with half-done drag makeup, contrasting sharply with the biting tone of his voice.

A perfect embodiment of a Libra—delicate, yet formidable.

"Get in here," he commanded, yanking me in and slamming the door shut behind us.

The penthouse was an open-concept wonderland of debauchery, like a Jackson Pollock painting if the artist were into BDSM. Casual sex swing in the corner, an assortment of cages, and leashes strewn about, it had a sort of twisted charm. And then there was the owner… or "the sub", a middle-aged guy hogtied in the corner with **Cash Slave** scrawled on his forehead like a walking billboard for financial masochism.

Bambi led me to a whiteboard with a numerical list of 'games' written in bold, garish colours.

He pointed, voice sharp with frustration. "We're at game twelve."

I squinted at it: **Ball's Eye. Fifteen bucks per hit.** "Subtle," I mused, my eyes darting to Bambi's Picasso-esque makeup. "Going for the abstract expressionist look?"

"Can we just get this over with?!" His eyes flicked like lit dynamite, as his voice screeched. "You're hours late, Vix!"

I grabbed an orange from a bowl on the table, aimed, and lobbed it at the sub's crotch, as he released a painful grunt.

Bull's eye.

"Awn, poor fucking baby can't handle a little orange? Pathetic," I taunted the sub.

I turned to Bambi, signalling for him to follow my lead, a smirk dancing across my lips.

Bambi stuttered, his words a clumsy ballet. "Yeah! You big ol' bitch… bi—boy—man?" he stammered, struggling to find his footing in this twisted game.

WTF was that, Sesame Street After Dark?

He was a soft soul, unused to the ever empowering vernacular of dom-play. I couldn't help but cringe.

"Some of us are nice people, Vixen. And not good at this shit," Bambi whispered back to me, noticing my unimpressed gaze.

I eyed the board once more. "Back Crack. If I make a sound, thirty bucks," I read off the board, my eyes already trailing to the sub, who crawled over as if summoned.

"And I have a freaking show at ten," Bambi groaned, running a hand through his hair.

Ignoring his panicked interjection, I leapt onto the sub's back, my boots connecting with a satisfying thud.

Bambi winced, his words rushing out in a nervous tumble, "I need this gig. Screw this up for me again, and I'm out of the drag world for good."

I lit a cigarette, swinging casually as the sub obediently knelt beside me. "I'm sorry! Geez. I got caught up this morning… but I got you. We'll wrap up this off-brand fifty shades and you'll be there on time."

"We better." Bambi shot back, glaring at me as he read the next game on the list, his face turning green.

His hand flew to his mouth and he turned away. "I'm gonna be sick."

At that moment, My phone buzzed, and **The Devil** flashed on screen. Again. I ignored it, sighing and flicking my cigarette ashes into the sub's eager mouth. The ember's crackling filled the room.

"How many games left?" I asked Bambi, who glared at me from the other side of the room, a whip in hand.

He let out a defeated sigh, the whip cracking against the floor in a display of faux defiance.

♡ SHUFFLE. SHUFFLE. ♡ DRAW.

"Where the hell is my money"

Bambi's apartment complex was a fossil, the hallway an archaeological dig into the malaise of mid-century decor. Peeling wallpaper hung from the walls like the fading dreams of a vintage starlet, the floorboards squealing beneath our boots as if they were the chorus of a grunge track. It was as if the place was rebelling against the very concept of walking, let alone strutting. The saddest of catwalks.

There I was, wobbling along this makeshift walkway, counting the cash I'd earned while Bambi fumbled with the keys to unit 221. He was close to a meltdown, the ticking clock his worst enemy.

"Oh. My. God, I'm gonna be SO late," His voice fluttered between exasperation and anxiety, fidgeting with the keys like a contortionist trying to untangle their limbs.

Unable to help my smirk, I was about to tease him when my eyes snagged on a sauntering enigma. Towering and symmetrical, he glided past us, his gaze intoxicating. Eyes like cerulean dreams, clear yet endlessly deep. A Marilyn Monroe beauty mark, positioned perfectly on his cheek, only added to his charm. He sipped a neon-green slushy, which in anyone else's hands would have looked like a toxic waste product but in his, seemed like ambrosia.

Gemini, for sure. Their allure has a way of acting like a gravitational pull—unclear yet undeniable.

His playful smirk clashed with my mesmerized frown, a spell woven and locked as he waltzed backward into his apartment, still sipping his Shrek juice. Those eyes of his remained riveted to mine until he was out of sight, leaving my spine buzzing with tingles.

Blue eyes. My fucking kryptonite.

"Come on!" I got jolted back from my reverie by Bambi's squeal, the door finally succumbing to his frantic fumbling. As if it, too, were saying, 'Fine! Just get in! Stop having a breakdown on my doorstep!'

With a final pull, the door gave way and he tugged me in, slamming it shut behind us. Severing the momentary connection with blue eyes.

Inside was a different universe entirely—a fever dream in pastels and LEDs. Plushies congregated in corners like secret meetings of the kawaii elite. A rainbow gaming station pulsed like the heart of a cybernetic organism, while a ring-lit iPhone stood poised for live-streaming fame. Where unicorn vomit meets angsty teen gamer.

Bambi, in his usual dramatic fashion, slammed his headphones down and strutted nervously to his vanity, leaving me to marvel at his gaming station.

"This is new—" I mused, my eyes lingering on the glow of the LED lights.

"Behold my empire," Bambi half-whispered, half-gasped, rummaging through his drawers with a clash of nervous energy. "You like? No, don't answer. I don't need validation… do you like it?"

I smirked and sauntered towards the mini-bar, adorned with an assortment of anime stickers, and poured myself an orange-tinted cocktail. The gin was heavy, just how I liked it. "It's... very you."

"Sick—Okay, paint me. NOW!" Bambi's voice pulled me from my drink.

My phone buzzed again.

INCOMING CALL FROM THE DEVIL

I chose to ignore it, taking a long sip from my cocktail instead.

"Another one?" Bambi inquired, removing his top as he prepared for the magic I was about to perform with my brushes.

I couldn't help but chuckle, dipping my brush into a pot of vivid pink eyeshadow and applying it onto Bambi's lids.

"What?" I retorted, feigning innocence.

"Another client?" Bambi's voice was laced with layers of irony and judgment, his reflection in the pink vanity mirror locking eyes with mine, daring me to contradict him.

"Bambi. You know it pays well." I defended myself, blowing gently on his painted eyelid. "It's not like you've never done it."

Bambi recoiled dramatically, "Excuse ME?! I've been out of service for a WHILE now."

He turned back to the mirror, a satisfied smile playing on his lips as he admired the work I'd done so far.

"You know damn well all I do is findom… and stream." His gaze fell onto me through the mirror. "There's a whole community ready to tip you, y'know. WITHOUT having to sell your soul to the streets."

As if on cue, my phone buzzed again.

INCOMING CALL FROM THE DEVIL

Bambi's eyes widened as he caught a glimpse of the caller ID. "Are you FREAKING kidding me?!"

I silenced him by answering the call, staying mute, waiting for the devil himself to speak.

"Took you a while—"

"What do ya want, Jay?" I interrupted him, "I'm a busy gal, Hun."

Jay's snarky laugh echoed from the other end, "Where the hell is my money."

My chuckle was cut short as I stood abruptly, knocking my cocktail, causing it to spill across the bar.

"Three months. We agreed on THREE months. I'm not a fucking charity." Jay's venomous voice echoed in my ears, disrupting the colourful tranquility of Bambi's apartment.

"Babe, I'll have it by—"

"The end of the week. Yeah. Cut the crap, Bitch. We've all heard it before."

I smirked, licking my teeth, and turned to Bambi who was watching our silent conversation, his eyes wide with fear.

"it's fine," I mouthed, shrugging off Jay's threats.

"What did you do?!" Bambi mouthed back, his eyes nearly bulging out of his sockets.

Jay continued his rant on the other end of the line, "I heard you took my cash and spent it on some fancy ass loft and a red fucking fur coat?!"

Red? Oh hell no.

At that, I couldn't help but giggle. "Jay, Hun, if you must know, your cash has been reincarnated into something far sexier—a burgundy—not red—fur coat," I purred, putting on my best Marilyn Monroe impression. "The boys really do love it." I twirled around, smirking, my movement causing my half-empty cocktail to spill over the edge of the bar.

"Listen BITCH. I'm sick of your FUCKING games! Get my FUCKING money. And get your ASS over here—" Jay snarled, an audio assault, all his pent-up venom discharging through the phone like poison darts. But I was made of kevlar and glitter.

"Byyyyye, Jay!" I hung up, downed my cocktail, and grabbed my tarot deck, ready to distract myself from his pathetic attempt of a threat.

"What the hell was that?!" Bambi practically shrieked, his eyes wide enough to rival saucers.

I laughed it off, "You prefer red or pink lips?"

Ignoring his pressing questions, I shuffled the deck with the dexterity of a Vegas dealer.

Shuffle, shuffle. Draw. **The Devil**. How fitting.

Bambi, ever the empath, wasn't ready to drop it, "VIXEN?!"

I flicked my wrist with dramatic flair. "Okay—fuck! I just spent a bit of Jay's cash. It's not a big deal." Shuffle, shuffle. Draw. **Justice**. "See? Tarot agrees. Justice for the Devil's deeds."

"I thought you 'exorcised' that pimp out?" Bambi's voice had hit an octave that even Mariah would envy.

Ignoring his anxiety-powered falsetto, I sloshed more gin into my glass, bypassing a cocktail umbrella because who has time for that? "Speaking of exorcism, did you know gin is practically holy water?" I wasn't interested in confessing the depths of my mistakes.

"How much?" Bambi cut in, his voice turning so serious, you'd think he was negotiating a peace treaty.

I stalled, stirring my fresh cocktail, not meeting his intense gaze.

"HOW. MUCH. VIXEN—" His voice grew louder, more insistent.

"Ten grand. It's fine, it's practically Monopoly money."

My nonchalant response elicited a flabbergasted reaction from Bambi, his perfectly manicured hand flying up to his forehead, nearly dislodging one of his meticulously glued-on rhinestones. "Goddamn it, Vix. Jay's got all the warmth and good intentions of a straight razor." He sighed, shaking his head. "This NEEDS to stop. I never trusted that prick. He's dangerous—"

What needs to stop is your over-the-top, My Little Pony fever dream of a colour palette.

Bambi sighed, his voice a cocktail of anxiety and pure exasperation. "Seriously, Vix! Your ex being your pimp is so fucked up. It's toxic. I get that he helped you out, but —"

"I can handle him." I reassured him, but Bambi wasn't convinced.

"I know you can, but geez… just cut him out. You know?" He implored, sighing deeply as he realized his words were falling on deaf ears.

"Like, stop with the bad boy thing. Heal. And who knows…" He shrugged, hoping to impart some wisdom, "You might even get into a healthy relationship—"

Abso-fucking-lutely not.

I chuckled nervously, "I don't want anyone."

"Of course you don't. All I'm saying… you can still escort. Jay's just a fuck twat." Bambi offered, desperate to help me see reason.

I grinned, completely unfazed."I've been doing it for three years. And you see? Nothing's happened to me. Still alive. Still fabulous." I argued, trying to lighten the mood, "As hot as ever actually—"

"YET. Keyword, nothing YET!" Bambi retorted, almost choking on his own desperation.

Tossing my head back, I swivelled away from his pleading eyes and waded through a closet that practically glowed with neon excess. "You sound like an infomercial for existential dread."

"Will you at least come tonight? Please?" His voice was softer now, more vulnerable. "The owner is real chill.

You might land a job as a server or something. It's basically escorting."

"Bambi. Love you to death, but no." I grabbed a sequin dress that screamed both diva and slightly unhinged. I dangled it in the air, my eyes meeting his. "Get dressed. It's high time your face had an outfit that matched its drama."

A reluctant smile broke through Bambi's fretful demeanour, as I turned back to the table where the tarot cards lay spread out. Among them, **The Devil** caught my eye again, as if it had summoned me for a private tête-à-tête. For a moment, I stared at it.

Bambi couldn't see it, and I'd never let him. But for a heartbeat, I felt **The Devil** whisper secrets only I could hear—about choices made and roads yet to travel. As much as I was the life of every party, every after-party, and every 'what the hell happened last night?' moment, that card told me there were debts to be settled.

"So," I muttered softly, only for myself and the Devil to hear, "are we dancing or are we duelling?"

As I scooped up the deck, sliding **The Devil** back into the motley lineup, my expression was a perfect mask of frivolity. But in the clandestine chambers of my thoughts, the dance was far from over. And I would decide the rhythm.

I could feel a tempest was brewing—and faster than my next cocktail mix.

♡ CERULEAN GAZE ♡
& MARILYN WAYS.

"I don't do dates"

The night enveloped me in its serene quietude as I glided out of Unit 221. "See ya, Hun" I trilled, sashaying my way into the anonymity of the night.

"Later, Boo!" Bambi's retort floated after me, cushioned by the solid click of the door. Suddenly, I was a solo act, parading through a dim corridor, its moody shadows interrupted by sporadically flickering bulbs—my own chiaroscuro runway. Like lighthouses lost in a storm. I always loved the quiet, the way the silence settled in and hummed along with my own heartbeat… but it was in those moments that darkness always crept in.

As I strutted down the hallway, a shiver crawled up my spine, uninvited. My thoughts went wild. Jay's voice echoed in my mind, the cruel edge of his words twisting to what he really meant: "You can run, Vixen, but you can never hide. Not from me." A cold fact, perhaps. But facts had never really been my thing. Life's too short for unwanted reruns, I reminded myself, shaking off the dread.

The Devil flashed before my eyes—a harbinger or a joke, who could tell?

Suddenly, a voice pierced the quiet, as unexpected as a bullet. "You a drag queen too?"

"FUCK!" I yelped, nearly ejecting myself from my combat boots. Spinning around, I locked eyes with a pair of cerulean blues, framed by an expression of sheepish curiosity.

My heart quickstepped against my ribs. Marilyn Monroe beauty mark. Bushy brows. Ah, Bambi's next-door Shrek-juice-drinking neighbour.

His apology came fast, but it couldn't slow my heartbeat. My eyes narrowed at him.

"Whoa—my bad," he chuckled, scratching his head, pointing to unit 221, "They've been going in and out frantically—with a wig on—for the past two days… just figured—"

"Hm. The residential stalker. Lovely," I retorted, a smirk tugging at the corner of my lips.

His laughter ringed out, an honest sound that echoed in the deserted corridor. "I prefer the term… neighbourhood watchdog," he replied, a self-appointed title that made me chuckle despite myself.

His smirk mirrored mine.

But it wasn't just a smirk—it was a silent narrative, rich with hidden agendas. The edge of his mouth twitched upwards, not quite reaching his eyes, as if he knew some cosmic joke and was deciding whether to let me in on it. That smirk was as disarming as it was compelling, hinting at a world of secrets. Even as a seasoned charmer who'd seen more faux smiles than a politician at a campaign rally, this one gave me pause. Was he intrigued? Amused? Up to something?

That smirk.

A handsome grin, "Quinn."

The name landed between us like an unspoken dare. In response, I offered a cryptic nod, pressing my lips together.

"Aaand you are?" he pressed, arching an eyebrow suggestively.

I hesitated, but not for long. "Vixen."

He pushed for more. "Real name. Not drag name… so this stalker can look you up on Insta."

He laughed at his own joke. Just when—

Ping!

 Drawing Quinn's attention. "Or PrideMate apparently."

I clarified, "I don't do drag. It's… just Vixen."

The admission lingered between us. His curiosity sparked my own. "Vixen. Cute. So, what's your game? Undercover superhero? Indie rockstar I don't know about or something—"

Time for the curveball.

"Escort… actually." I threw the word out there like a grenade, waiting for the smoke to rise and for him to vanish in it. But he just blinked, and that world-illuminating smile stayed firmly in place. "Interesting. Very interesting," he said.

Huh.

I expected a clattering of moral high heels by now, or at the very least, a look of thinly veiled judgment. Most guys hear 'escort,' and suddenly they have an 'urgent appointment' they forgot about.

His eyes held mine, and there was something in his gaze, something that made my heart beat a little faster. The grin that spread across his face was almost infectious.

"I respect the hustle," he said, those eyes locked onto mine.

"The hustle?" Is he for real? Is he actually unfazed or just a hell of an actor?

"What? Expected me to clutch my pearls?" He added.

Oh, he's got jokes now?

Hun, if you had pearls, they'd be mine already. But I didn't say that. I couldn't. I was too busy spiralling down the rabbit hole of 'what does this mean?'

"So you're not just a cutie with a tattooed smirk." I wanted to say it out loud, to test the waters more, but my thoughts tangled with my words. "You've got depth. Layers." Like an onion? Or a truffle—rich and a bit intoxicating, I'd retort.

What's wrong with me.

But his laugh filled the air instead, that sound of genuine enjoyment, and I was there mentally dissecting the moment like it was a scene in a Shakespearean drama—where I had forgotten my lines, but the other actor was so damn good he was carrying the show.

"Well, Vixen, consider me intrigued," he said, and suddenly, it was not about intrigue, it was about me feeling like the prey in a chase I had always led. A sensation I hadn't thought I'd want until then.

For the first time in God knows when, I was the one tempted by the apple, not the serpent offering it.

"Well—see ya," I dismissed him, ready to retreat back into the comfort of solitude. But he was not done.

"How 'bout we get some drinks?" he called after me.

"I don't do dates," I returned, my gaze already drifting.

"Right. Right…" He trailed off, pulling out his phone, his fingers dancing across the screen.

Ping!

A PrideMate notification.

(Quinn): **What's your hourly rate**? A challenge.

"How about now," Quinn teased.

I blushed, a heat creeping up my neck. My hourly rate. Funny. The question floated in the digital space between us. And I typed back:

(Me): **Guess ya know where to find me.**

He looked up, locking eyes with me. Our smirks met like a mirror's reflection. I pivoted and strutted away, leaving him standing in the moody hallway. I could feel his eyes still on me. The night was silent once more, except for the thumping of my own heartbeat. As I turned the corner, I let out a breath I hadn't realized I'd been holding. A breath tinged with unexpected anticipation.

Pff… what a weirdo…

♡ THE SPANDEX ♡ STILETTO TRAIN WRECK.

"Try squeezing in pilates between
a bachelorette brunch and Drag-con"

The straightest medley of metallic clangs and self-satisfied grunts played on loop, a questionable Spotify playlist for my morning pump. This gym—a monument to blandness, the elevator music of fitness palaces. Imagine a room painted in shades of disinterest, then sprinkle in a dash of mediocrity—and you've got this hellhole.

I glistened, practically marinating in my own sweat, as I wound down my treadmill routine. The machine's final sighs harmonized with my heartbeat, culminating in a sort of exhausted symphony. Just as I was poised to change the soundtrack of my morning—a curtain call, if you will—my phone chimed in with a dramatic entrance of its own.

Ping!

PrideMate; how quaint.

(DimDad84): **Heya. You do high-end events?**

My eyes glanced around the room, searching… finally resting on a forty-something man, engrossed in his phone as if decoding nuclear launch codes. Our eyes locked. A timid grin crept across his lips, as though he'd just solved a particularly challenging crossword clue.

I reciprocated with a smirk that was half-charm, half-warning—like saying, "You're cute, but tread carefully, darling"—before my fingers took to the keyboard like Liberace on a grand piano.

(Me): **Can you afford them?**

I tapped out, throwing my gauntlet into the virtual ring, leaving a seductive gaze behind.

The locker room was a vivid collage of tired testosterone, stale sweat, and regrettable life choices. Amidst the clang of lockers and the one saggy gentleman letting his bits dangle as if mistaking the gym for a bathhouse, I was all jazz-hands, shoving my duffle bag to the brim.

But—there came Dame Diva Disaster in baby-pink spandex leggings, platform heels, and an expression that could have given a mirror a mid-life crisis. This glamor-toad, sporting half a makeup war zone on her face, sidled next to me, huffing like a locomotive with bronchitis.

"'Scuse me, Sugar," her voice drawled, with a Southern twist.

My eyes quickly tangoed, zeroing in on her leggings, and it was a full-on horror show down there.

"Try squeezing in pilates between a bachelorette brunch and Drag-con. It ain't easy," she said, eyes meeting mine.

Ping!

(DimDad84): **250 for 2 hours?**

(Me): **Make it 300, and I'll be extra cute**

The antediluvian drag queen, eavesdropping with the stealth of a tank, purred with a cigarette-husky voice, "Oh, sweetheart…"

Ping!

(DimDad84): **See you tonight. 8 PM. 12 Rachel E**

"Need anything?" I shot back, catching her eye.

"You can do better than cruising the gym for a couple bucks. Look at you. Monetize, Sugar, monetize," she advised.

My fingers gripping my phone a little tighter. "That isn't really any of your concern, Sir—"

Cutting me off, "That's Emma Royd to you, love."

I couldn't help but grimace in response.

Ew.

"As in a pain in the ass?" I taunted.

Her laugh rung out, a cackle layered over decades of smoke and sass. "Oh, shut up. Ya love it."

She lit a cigarette, the aroma spiralling up like some phantom of gym etiquette long since murdered. "It hasn't changed one bit ya know. Those streets are still a freaking death trap," she said, almost nostalgically.

I ignored her, continuing to pack my bag.

"And what are ya gonna do after this gig? Huh? Back home? Spend all that cash as fast as you can? Then back to cruising?" She stared me down.

I shut her out, slamming my locker, and quickly packed my belongings, glaring her down. "You got it, Sir."

Her laughter followed me, tinged with a smoker's cough, as I continued. "I don't need the advice of some off-brand Lady Bunny," I retorted, sealing my locker like a vault of secrets.

"Maybe," she hacked out a cough, "but I've seen the high and lows, Sugar. You won't be a twinkling star forever." She aimed her cigarette at me. "That attitude'll get ya the high life for a few years, but the second those good looks disappear… you'll be rotting on the streets— alone."

Her words reverberated like an echo in a hollow chamber. They were accusations, assumptions that stung more than I would have liked to admit. My silence didn't deter her. "Trust me. I'd know," she inhaled her cigarette, "Wouldn't wish it on my worst enemy—"

The smell invaded my senses, and I couldn't help but interject, pointing to her cigarette, "You can't smoke in here."

She laughed, "It's a fake cigarette. I'm being dramatic, Sugar."

She was relentless. I couldn't deny the small part of me that appreciated her frankness, her authenticity.

"Runaway, eh? Left it all behind at eighteen. Fled to the city…"

My teeth grinded against each other.

She went on, "Met a guy? Probably worked out for a while… but quickly turned to shit when he started to rent ya out to other rats?"

Fuck you, Bitch.

I clenched my jaw, about to lose my shit. "A brick wall eh… Bambi was right about ya," she continued, her voice echoing in the nearly empty locker room.

"Of course, he put you up to this," I said, the words slipping out in a frustrated sigh.

She pushed a hot pink business card into my hands. '**Loving Jacqueline**', it read, punctuated with little hearts and wobbly-legged figures in heels.

I scoffed, tauntingly. "Bambi's gigs are in a brothel?"

She leaned in, her eyes narrowing. "What happens behind the curtain ain't none of Bambi's biz." She walked past me, patting my shoulder on her way out. "If you're looking for a new stage, the door's always open. There's plenty of money to be made."

With a swish of her feathered scarf, she was gone, leaving me in a fog of layered contradictions.

I looked down at the card in my hand, as a feeling of uncertainty washed over me. Indignation? and Curiosity? Those little fishnet legs taunting me with their obnoxious kitsch glitter heels.

Flicking my wrist, I chucked the card into the nearest trash bin and rolled my eyes.

Fuck that.

♡ DESIGNER DISASTERS. ♡
& DINOSAUR DALLIANCES.

"You look like a fucking clown"

The Polov Hotel Benefit was a garish display of excess, glimmering under lights, the aura of the one percent—a charade for the trust-fund babies and the tax-evading dinosaurs. I slinked through the crowd, targeting Dimitri, that monument to silver-fox manhood from the gym.

His disdain hit me immediately, eyes narrowing at my attire.

Geez. A little skin never killed anyone. Geez.

Before Dimitri so 'eloquently' dissected my wardrobe choices, I had been quite fond of my ensemble for the night. Honestly, how could you go wrong with leather pants so tight they could qualify as a second skin? They were the kind of pants that told the world, "Yes, I'm here to break your heart and probably your furniture." Add to that a mesh shirt that was equal parts 'runway chic' and 'back alley fight club.'

The shirt was a designer piece, mind you—a treasure from a brand you'd need to buy vowels to pronounce. But the avant-garde artistry of it, paired with the low-brow grit of my pants, gave off the vibe of 'expensive garbage,' like a dumpster filled with champagne bottles and caviar tins.

Tacky? Maybe. But there's a fine line between tasteless and fearless, and I was dancing all over it, heels and all.

I forced a smile, lips curling into my signature grin, as I sashayed his way. Just when—

He yanked me behind some decorative flora, looking for all the world like a man in deep regret. "What the hell is this?" he hissed.

"This, Hun, is designer," I shot back, giving my coat a little flip for added drama.

"Yeah, well you look like a fucking clown," Dimitri retorted. "What do you see?" He gestured towards the crowd of overripe, moneyed old men.

I smirked, a wicked twist of my lips, gesturing at the sea of bald spots and combovers. "A lineup for palliative care?"

"Investors. Politicians," he corrected, barely containing his annoyance. "You look like a fucking hooker. Get outta here—"

Taken aback, my eyes widened. "Hey! Hun…I-I can just take the coat off—look," I argued, removing my coat hastily. "There. Coat's off. We good?"

I tried to drape my arms around his neck in what I imagined to be a seductive fashion. He wasn't buying it.

"So, when's your birthdate—" I started, but he abruptly pulled my hands away from him.

His grip was harsh, squeezing my wrists tightly. I laughed, trying to defuse the tension.

"Oh. We playing kinky now, Daddy?" I teased, but Dimitri was having none of it.

With an unexpected force, he pushed me to the ground. "GET OFF ME! YOU FUCKING WHORE!"

The hard, ornate tile of the Polov Hotel's terrace met my back with a cold, unyielding embrace. I felt the intricate patterns of the mosaic digging into my skin, the chill from the ground seeping through the fabric of my clothes.

His words cut through the night air, leaving me sprawled on the ground, dumbstruck. I glared up at him, my jaw clenching as I tried to control my anger.

I picked myself up, the mosaic patterns imprinted temporarily on my skin. "Yeah—well, whatever, I don't do expired twinks anyways," I sneered back at him.

He rolled his eyes, his laughter bitter and cold, as he walked away without another word, calling back: "Get out before I call the cops."

I stood up, dusting myself off.

Jackass.

Licking my lips, I looked around, my mind whirling as my heart pounded in my chest. Anger welled up in me, replacing the embarrassment of Dimitri's rejection. My fingers flew across my phone screen, updating my PrideMate headline: **!LOOKING NOW!$$**

Waiting, I tapped my foot on the ground, an impatient drumroll in the silence that followed. Anger boiled within me, hot and urgent. Then, as if on cue—

Ping!

I grinned. The night was still young, after all.

♡ HEART OF GLASS. ♡

"Just go with it. Don't be a sissy"

Amidst the devilish crimson glow of my loft, the heart-shaped neon sign bathed the room in scandalous shades of red, turning my sanctuary into a hazy harem of lucid dreams. Connie Smith's "Burning a hole in my mind" reverberated through the air, the beat intermingling with the exhilarating buzz of MDMA—my trusty little pink pill acolyte—rushing through my veins.

Cocktail in hand, I moved in a hypnotic sway, my red fur coat whispering against my skin. The taste of orange bursting on my tongue, the potent mix already had me on a high. The ice cubes in my glass clinked like rebellious wind chimes, each note orchestrating the dance of the heart-shaped nipple covers donned with audacious flair on my bare chest, the signature provocative addition.

The world seemed blurred, laughter spilling from my lips when—

A sudden buzz interrupted my merriment at the door. I opened to find, my PrideMate date, Clyde, standing awkwardly. His muscular build intimidating, like a modern-day Greek god. A thick moustache covered his upper lip, giving him a rugged, almost raw appeal.

Mmm, Zaddy.

"You Vixen?" His voice was more of a low growl, sending shivers down my spine.

I offered him a teasing smile and a nod, an unspoken invitation.

His eyes took a detour to my chest. "Nice tits."

Charming. Another grunting neanderthal with the complexity of a drywall.

"Thanks?… Hun," I managed to say, my voice holding a hint of disdain as I pulled him into the apartment, leading him to my faux-leather, avant-garde throne, also known as my couch.

"You from here?" I probed, laying the groundwork for whatever emotional entrapment was necessary to make this rendezvous bearable.

His nod was less expressive than a parking meter.

"When's your birthdate?" I continued, fishing for details to unravel him.

"Uh... May sixteen," he paused, confused.

Careful now. Might blow a blood vessel.

"Nineteen eighty one," he sluggishly clarified.

I forced a smirk, licking my upper lip. Adding up my ammunition together. "Mmh... Taurus!"

Ah, a Taurus with the conversational depth of a cereal box. "Libra moon, too," I said, casting my astrological net, gleaning insights for my subsequent manipulations.

"So, what's the plan here, big guy?" I arched back, emphasizing the teasing tone I'd mastered through years of experience.

Clyde wasted no time unbuckling his belt. "Well-Um..." he cleared his throat, "My wife won't find out about this right?"

As if on cue, I erupted into a giggle that carried a subtle note of madness, slowly brushing my arm across the crevasses of my leather couch. Lost in the cold sensation.

Definitely too much MDMA.

Staring at the couch, I whispered, "Dance with me."

I sprung up eyes closed, waltzing towards Clyde, and opened them to him—fully nude and... expectant. Catching me off guard.

"Fuck! Okay... that's a—an interesting shape—" My comment was cut off when he gripped me by my waist, forcefully spinning me around, his body crashing into mine.

He slammed me against the window. There was a roughness to his touch, an urgency that bordered on violence.

"Easy, daddy!" I tried to slow things down. Something felt off. A shift in the air, a darkening of the mood. He slid his hands down my leather pants. Feeling me up. Which, don't get me wrong, was kind of the point... but something wasn't right.

"Heya—no rush here—", I added.

My warning alarms started ringing when his hands abandoned my waist, migrating instead to my throat, squeezing. Nails digging into my skin.

Not. The fucking. Throat.

Ice. Cold. Fear. Memories I'd buried started to surface, fight-or-flight kicking in. My eyes darted across the room for some type of makeshift lifeline. When—

My Tiffany lamp.

"Hun. Stop. Not there," my voice wavered, each word punctuated by an increasing struggle for breath, as I reached out for my Tiffany lamp.

"Shh. It's fine." Clyde's dismissive murmur tried to muffle my growing desperation.

I desperately kept reaching out, panic in my eyes, "I'm not… fucking around," I hissed, the struggle to breathe becoming more pronounced.

His gaze hardened. "Just go with it. Don't be a sissy."

Gotcha.

In a surge of adrenaline, I seized my Tiffany lamp, my grip tightening. And, in true 'flip-fuck fashion', I reversed Clyde, sandwiching him to the window, while repeatedly bashing him against it. Fracturing the glass panes upon every stroke of impact.

"I TOLD YOU, NOT THE FUCKING THROAT," I bellowed, my voice a cocktail of fury and trauma.

And then, I struck. In a surge of adrenaline, I swung my Tiffany lamp in a high arc and slammed it against Clyde's skull. Colourful shards exploded across the room, the sound echoing like a gunshot.

Clyde, reeling from the impact, swayed unsteadily on the spot, his eyes clouded with shock and disbelief. For a moment, he seemed lost, trying to register what had just happened. Clutching his throbbing head with one hand, he used the other to blindly grope for his coat, his fingers trembling.

He glanced back at me one last time, his expression a mix of anger, confusion, and fear. "You're fucking crazy!" he spat, his voice shaky. Without another word, he staggered out, struggling with the door for a brief second before he managed to pull it open and disappeared into the hallway.

I was left alone, surrounded by the afterglow of my scarlet sanctuary and the neon sign's soft hum.

Alone but not defeated, I stared at my fractured window. "Yeah… that's my brand," I whispered to myself, my eyes wet with a mixture of tears and smudged eyeliner.

Half-naked, catching my breath, I moved closer, touching the glass cracks as if they were a reflection of my own fragmented soul. And looked through it—

The ground below beckoned, drawing my gaze inexorably downward. From three stories up, everything looked distant, distorted, detached. People moved like miniature figurines, shadows in the rain. They seemed so remote, so alien, existing in a different world than my sanctuary high above.

It was vertigo—not just from the height, but from the surrealness of it all. Suspended in mid-air, I felt like Rapunzel, trapped in her tower—except my prison was of my own making.

The dizziness was overwhelming. Each time I peered down, it felt as if the ground was surging up to meet me, calling me in its embrace. It whispered secrets of freedom, of oblivion, of escape from the relentless cycle of hurt.

I shook that off quickly.

Rather, glancing up one last time at that insistent neon sign. Its buzzing seemed to fill the space between my ears, almost like a chant, a mantra. LOVE. LOVE. LOVE. Mocking me. Mocking what I sold.

With a trembling hand, I removed one of my heart-shaped nipple covers and used it to patch the centre of the shattered window, forcing a smile onto my face—a smile that was half brick wall, half surrender. Teetering on the edge of breaking.

Then my phone lit up.

(Bambi): **Come. I need your help**.

I stared at the text, my heart still racing, the neon light casting a kaleidoscope of emotions over my reflection. But there was no time for that.

And off I went.

♡ THE DEVIL. ♡

"Two weeks, Vixen. Or bodies start disappearing"

I sluggishly entered Bambi's apartment. "Heya, Babe. What's wrong—"

There was an ominous, almost eerie, aura. The LED lights of his gaming station flashed like a disco in hell, slicing through the inky darkness as I tiptoed inside. "Bambi?"

I turned the corner and what met my eyes was a tableau from the worst of nightmares—

Bambi, sprawled across the floor, his body bruised and battered like a marionette in some sadist's puppet show. Two shadows loomed ominously, their features swallowed by the darkness. And then my eyes locked onto the puppet master—a snarling, grimy figure who looked like Tommy Lee if Tommy Lee had a blue-haired demon twin, grinning like a fiend with a knife gleaming menacingly to Bambi's throat.

My heart plummeted.

There, standing like a malevolent force, was Jay.

He was a calamity in human form...

Looking like he'd just crawled out of an underground punk show and landed in our lives. He was lean, almost skinny, but his presence weighed heavy, filling the room like dark matter. Tattoos swirled around his arms, up his neck, and disappeared under the ragged white tank top he wore. Each inked design seemed like a chapter in a story you didn't want to read. His electric-blue hair contrasted sharply with the darker elements of his persona, but don't let the playful colour fool you. His eyes were cold, cutting through you like the blade he carried—both equally deadly. Jay was the sort of guy you'd cross the street to avoid, and for good reason.

He sneered, a gleam of sadistic delight playing across his face. "Took you long enough."

I fought to steady my quivering voice. "What the FUCK, Jay?"

His laughter grated on my nerves. "After all I did for you?" he drawled, prowling closer like a predator who knew its prey was cornered. "The money. The attention. Getting rid of that creep."

His eyes, cold and calculating, danced between Bambi and me. When his fingers tightened around Bambi's face, my heart constricted in my chest. "Don't test my generosity, doll," he hissed.

I shuffled my feet nervously, eyes falling to my boots. "I wonder how much this little doe would sell for..." Jay mused, his voice dripping with dark amusement as his knife's edge grazed Bambi's throat. "Probably enough to settle your debts?"

"Don't you fucking DARE!" The words erupted, shattering my veneer of indifference.

Jay laughed, a sickeningly sweet sound. "Is this one special to you?" he cooed, taunting me.

I bit back a retort, my lips forming a tight line.

"Here I was thinking you were always a lone wolf," Jay continued, each word like a cut, "but you're just another fucking softie. All bark, no bite."

"I have your money," I stammered, desperate to lead him away from Bambi. "Ju—just give me a couple of weeks. Leave Bambi out of it. Please."

Jay smirked, a cruel contortion of his lips, as if thinking he had unearthed my Achilles heel. "So you do have a weakness." He kissed Bambi's forehead. "Who would've thought."

Forehead kisses—a hallmark of affection, the kind you'd expect from protective fathers or doting lovers. But the way Jay's lips met Bambi's skin was a calculated act. It was less a promise of protection and more a declaration of ownership, a brand seared without fire but with cold, calculated intent.

He wasn't just marking his territory; he was asserting his dominion over us both. 'Look at me,' those lips whispered without words, 'I can touch what's yours, and you can't do shit about it.'

He released Bambi and strode toward me, his boots thudding on the hardwood. "Two weeks, Vixen. Or bodies start disappearing."

His fingers wrapped around my throat, triggering an avalanche of suppressed fears and memories. I stifled my tears, standing firm.

"GOT IT?!" he roared like a madman.

I nodded, each movement sending spikes of pain through my neck. Choking out a feeble "got it."

"Good boy," he purred, his lips almost touching my cheek as he sauntered out of the apartment, his goons trailing behind like his personal demons.

I stared at the empty doorway for a brief instant, the taste of fear bitter in my mouth, before dropping to my knees beside Bambi, my eyes scanning his injuries. "Bambi, I'm sorry. Are you okay? What did he—"

"What the FUCK, Vix?!" Bambi screamed, shattering the silence. I met his eyes. "I'm so sorry. I won't let him hurt you. I promise," I murmured, pulling him into an embrace, his tears wetting my chest.

"How the HELL are you gonna get ten grand in TWO WEEKS?" Bambi's muffled words seared through me, branding each syllable into my soul.

How the actual fuck, indeed.

♡ LOVING JACQUELINE'S. ♡

"I charge extra for that"

The atmosphere in Jacqueline's was an opulent dystopia bathed in hedonistic splendour. A decadent club of iniquity, a fusion of Amsterdam's Red light District & Paris' Moulin Rouge. I sauntered in, the red velvet curtains parting like the Red Sea, but for a more diabolical Moses. My eyes drank in the lavish scenery: ornate rococo lampshades casting illicit silhouettes on the walls, golden metal grids outfitted with the most artisanal leather cuffs money could buy. God, the place even smelled like an aristocrat's orgy—French perfume mingling with delicious whispers of secrets best left untold.

The gatekeeper of this devilish haven was none other than Angel, and oh, what a paradox she was. A spectral vision of ethereal trans beauty and punk rebellion. Legs for days and smoky eyes that screamed high-fashion nihilism. Long, inky-black hair framed a face that perpetually looked like it was deciding between scorn and subterfuge. Her eyes—those scrutinizing orbs—were permanently etched with a look that couldn't decide between 'I'll burn your house down' or 'I already did.' Decked out in a macabre uniform of gothic punk and swatches of pink latex that screamed BDSM chic, she was an aesthetic contradiction. A visual riddle without an answer.

And then there was the tattoo—her most ironically sentimental body art—a dainty heart just below her eye. Given her vibe, one could be forgiven for wondering whether that heart represented lost love or the organ she'd carve out of your chest given half the chance.

Angel clocked me and blew a bubble with her gum.

Bubble gum pop!

Bursting it in a resounding pop that echoed through the room like a sinner's first step in hell. "You lost, Babs?" She teased, her eyes leisurely scanning me up and down as she blew another defiant bubble of gum.

Bubble gum pop!

"I'm here for Emma," I quipped, flicking the fringe of my red fur coat with melodramatic flair, with a smug smirk curling at the corners of my lips. "Babs."

Her eyes sparkled with mischief.

Bubble gum pop!

Every time she popped her bubble gum, which was incessantly, it felt like a warning shot.

The corners of her mouth twitched ever so slightly, her eyes flickering with a spark of reluctant admiration. With an almost dismissive flick of her perfectly stiletto manicured fingers, she leaned into the vintage phone. "MAMA, some bitch is here for you," as she returned to her magazine without a second glance, the very picture of nonchalance.

Before I could savour my impatience, a voice boomed from behind the curtain, echoing through the chamber. "Jesus! Play nice Angel—"

Entered Emma Royd, looking like she just stomped out of an old Hollywood screen test, if the screen test were for 'Mommie Dearest.' She eyed me, sizing me up as if she was debating whether I was a legitimate business opportunity or merely cannon fodder.

"Oh. You," she breathed, her voice dripping with acid-sweet resignation. Emma's gaze trailed over my red fur coat, and I could almost hear her internal scoff. "Alright… come in," she declared, punctuating her invite with a dramatic sweep of her arm, disappearing behind the curtain.

I chuckled, my heart racing in the most delightful way. God, I loved a room with tension thick enough to slice with a stiletto. Tripping lightly on my own sense of delicious irony, I followed her behind the curtain, curious about this so-called club.

The private boudoir was a spectacle, a blend of outdated glamour and ostentatious vulgarity. Ensconced in a cocoon of lush burgundy fur under a faux diamond chandelier, Emma Royd presided over her kingdom. Leopard print ashtray in hand, cigarette poised between her lips, she was the queen of this 1970s time capsule—a nostalgia trip of a room where the gaudy and the grandiose held court.

With a fluid grace that barely masked her entitlement, Emma sunk into an absurdly low chair, igniting her cigarette. I scanned the room, my lips curling in a grimace, much to Emma's amusement.

"Oh. Cause you're so high class?" she chortled, savouring her cigarette like it was a fine vintage. "I take it you're here for my offer?"

She was a relic of old Hollywood glamour, but the kind that never made it past the golden era—stuck in a time loop of vintage decadence. Her wig was a flaming red, styled into waves that should have been immortalized in black and white film. She wore her makeup thick, eyes dramatic and lips a bold rouge, framing a face that had seen things you wouldn't believe.

My nod affirmed her suspicion.

Emma looked me up and down, eyes narrowing. "It's pretty cut-and-dry. Ya get clients, ya indulge their fantasies—within reason, 'course—all for the right price. Can ya handle that, Sugar?"

As I parted my lips to speak—

Ping!

My phone erupted, a PrideMate notification splashing across the screen. Emma shot me a glare that could wilt roses.

"And none of that freelance bullcrap while you're on my payroll," she cautioned.

"What's the cut?" I asked, eager to establish terms.

"Straight to business… " Emma smiled, flicking her cig into the ashtray. "Sixty-forty—"

"As if," I interrupted, a wolfish grin curling my lips. "Seventy-thirty."

She laughed, her cackle interspersed with bouts of coughing. "Ya don't beat around the bush—"

"Actually… " I retorted, the smirk never leaving my face, "I charge extra for that."

"Clever girl." A twinkle appeared in Emma's eyes, a spark kindled by our mutual love for audacity. "Fine, seventy-thirty it is. Pleasure doing business with ya."

Leaning casually against the door frame, I flashed her a victorious smile. But the interrogation wasn't over.

"Ya don't have any unpaid pimps lingering around, do ya?" Emma inquired, the glow of her cigarette reflecting in her piercing gaze. "We don't take gals that already have a price on their head. Puts the whole flock at risk."

Don't let the washed-up diva act fool you; Emma had a business spark in her eyes that outshone any marquee.

She'd turned her drag queen allure into a brothel empire, wearing her 'Queen Bee' title like a diamond tiara. And while she seemed fiercely loyal to her girls, that loyalty clearly had its limits. Cross her or threaten the hive, and she'd cut you out without a second thought, as ruthlessly as she cut her own wigs. She was all business, and in her world, you either played your part, or you got played.

I shook my head in response, fiddling with my nails to avoid her scrutinizing stare.

"Good." Satisfied, she exhaled a lungful of smoke, the grey plume curling around her like a cloak. "Welcome to the club."

As I was about to exit her sanctum, she called out, "And keep the name, Vixen. It's got a good ring to it."

I reached for my pack of cigarettes, and in the clumsy shuffle, my MDMA capsules cascaded onto the floor.

"First client's in room six. Angel will show you," Emma's voice drenched in a sudden cold professionalism as her eyes settled on the fallen pills. "Do what ya gotta do, Sugar."

With a shrug that was both casual and calculated, I swept my scattered vices back into my pocket and sauntered out. I was Vixen, a hurricane in a human form, about to churn through the tempestuous sea that was Emma Royd's empire. Welcome to the club...

Jacqueline's dance floor was a visual bacchanal—gold chain chandeliers dangled from the ceiling like opulent spiderwebs, oversized golden birdcages hovered, and the crowd pulsated in a technicolor frenzy, an animated peacock tail set to a heavy beat. The atmosphere was an outrageous cocktail: one part Paris Red Light opulence, two parts Berghain's flagrant hedonism. I gulped down my trusty pink pill and, with a blissful grimace, hurled myself into the hypnotic anarchy.

"So professional," a voice sneered, with a tone rivalling even my own innate sass.

Emerging from the fringes, like the proverbial serpent in Eden, Angel slid up beside me. Her eyes—a masterclass in disdain—latched onto me. Dressed in gothic-punk finery, her pink latex outfit clung to her like a second skin, as unapologetically bold as the gum she chewed.

Bubble gum pop!

"Let's go." Guiding me to the bar, Angel gestured at Aspen and Kitty, who were concocting neon beverages with the flair of alchemists. "Aspen and Kitty. You'll be working pretty close together." Her voice dripped with venom, a black mamba in human form. Was it jealousy? Fear? Or just good, old-fashioned spite?

Kitty, a petite powerhouse with an effervescent energy. Her slender frame, punctuated by gracefully curved hips and a dainty waist, stood in high-wattage contrast to Aspen's bulk. With her vivid orange bob cascading down to her shoulders and her perpetually present cherry lollipop, she looked like the poster child for some twisted, over-sexualized, Akihabara anime store.

Aspen, on the other hand, with his chiseled jawline, broad shoulders, and a physique that looked like he lived at the gym, shot me a glare that screamed 'toxic gay-for-pay jock.' This potent blend of suspicion and territoriality was framed by his slightly too-tight club shirt, which seemed intent on displaying every sinew and contour of his sculpted torso.

I quipped, "Angry. Disgusted by everything. Violently judging everyone... my my, Aries never looked so good." Aspen's nostrils flared; mission accomplished.

Kitty's eyes widened at the sight of my red fur coat as though she'd just stumbled upon a unicorn, "OH MY GOD! I love your coat—"

Before Kitty's fingertips could sully my couture, I pirouetted away. "Eyes, not hands, Libra."

Behind the bar, I seized the gin bottle with the authority of a ship captain claiming new lands and mixed my cocktail, barely acknowledging the threesome's collective scowl. Turned to Angel, I played my signature siren song. "So, Avril Lavigne, when's your birth—"

She interjected, "The club's open Thursday to Saturday. And the Drag queens perform on Fridays"

Bubble gum pop!

Her gaze was almost glacial when she continued, bubble gum pop resonating in the background like her personal soundtrack. "The queens do their thing, and… " She glanced at Kitty and Aspen, "We do ours. Got it?"

I nodded along, pouring myself an orange cocktail. "No one ever gets suspicious?"

Bubble gum pop!

Angel turned around and smirked. "You think anyone hears anything over the music?"

Kitty's gleeful voice broke the tension. "You like dancing?!" Her eyes, twin galaxies of excitement, guided me to the solitary pole on the stage—a gleaming totem to all things glittery and sinful.

My body tingled with a cocktail of anticipation and recklessness. "Oh, Hun," I exclaimed, downing the rest of my drink. "The star of the show."

Angel's lips twisted into a grin that felt as genuine as a three-dollar bill. "Good, you'll make us some extra cash on pole duty then."

With one swift movement, she snatched my glass, placed it on the counter, and pointed to a waxy red door. "However… that right there is where the real money bleeds."

Angel's eyes studied me like I was a puzzle she couldn't quite solve. Or maybe a puzzle she didn't care to solve. Either way, she had put me on notice.

I stared at the door, my pulse ringing in my ears like an insistent drumbeat. I swallowed hard, momentarily unnerved. Right, this was what I signed up for—wasn't it?

♡ ASTRO-HOE-LOGY. ♡

"When's your birthdate?"

The hallway was an electric symphony of muffled giggles and throaty moans, each door a portal to a thousand bizarre fantasies. The walls throbbed in hues of green neon, like some sort of erotic Northern Lights. As I walked, the little pink pill began to weave its magic, each breath I drew seemed thicker. The MDMA coursing through my veins amplified the surreal landscape, dialling up the colours, the sounds, the pounding of my heart until it became a manic drum solo. My steps became an intoxicated dance, half-prowl, half-waltz.

"So, who's my guy?" I purred, unable to keep the playful lilt from my voice. "Closet case? Wall Street big-shot with a BDSM fetish?" My laugh ricocheted off the walls, a hollow sound that died under Angel's impassive

gaze. I swallowed, feigning innocence. "Oh God, not a...
widow?"

Angel's long black hair swung as she shook her head,
her voice a serrated knife. "It's a miracle you ever made
any cash."

I glided my fingertips over the vintage wallpaper, the
texture sending a tingling jolt up my spine. "Oh, please!
Everyone loves a playful kitty cat." I crooned, my world
lurching slightly as the high spiralled into a dizzying
crescendo. I couldn't help but sway to the imaginary beat,
the world reduced to a myriad of sensations. "So how
much per hour?"

"One-fifty," she droned.

I sucked in a sharp breath. Fuck.

Bambi'll be wild game at that rate.

My eyes widened, "That's not enough."

"House rules," Angel replied, a perfectly arched
eyebrow challenging my bravado. "You sure you're up for
this?" She smirked, "Remember, clients first—"

"I've been doing this longer than you've been popping
bubble gum, Hun," I snapped, though a nagging ripple of
doubt tried to surface from the depths.

Finally, we arrived at door number six. Angel's eyes narrowed, a fierce glare that told me to shut up without uttering a syllable. I saw my reflection in the lacquered door—a distorted circus mirror image of jittery eyes and clenched jaw. Shaking off the nerves, I caressed my fur coat and pivoted elegantly. "I'd give you a free class, but the show's about to start."

And with that flamboyant declaration, I twirled into the room, ready to conquer whatever or whoever lay beyond that door.

Sin and pleasure—Jacqueline's backrooms weren't exactly the Ritz-Carlton. Rather, they were sordid salons of secrecy, the kind of place your conscience warned you about but your desires demanded you enter. In short, they were tailor-made for someone like me: the glamorous misfit on the verge of an incandescent debut.

The room beckoned with satin allure, bedecked in leather and hazy green neon—each flicker a lingering sigh from the ghosts of affairs past. Empty bottles of massage oil whispered stories of ecstasy as they idled beside a tub frothing with intent. An ornate chandelier, though not on, hung from the ceiling, its crystal prisms catching the neon rays and scattering them, creating a soft, dreamlike sparkle.

And there sat Daryl. He looked like a lamb awaiting his slaughter—a walking cliché of trembles and awkward glances.

His body was a mess of contradictions. On one hand, he was textbook bashful, with a posture that could only be described as a folding chair in the midst of collapsing. His eyes darted around the room, anywhere but my face, as if the floor had suddenly become the most interesting piece of architecture. But despite his skittish demeanour, he was not unattractive. He had a disarming sort of innocence, a face that hadn't yet met the harsh realities of the world. Broad shoulders and strong arms contradicted his timid nature, suggesting that, given the right set of circumstances, he could be someone else entirely. His nervousness wasn't just palpable, it was practically its own entity, crowding the room. A raw cocktail of fear, excitement, and something deeper, perhaps regret or pain. I had always been good at this, at tuning into the unseen frequencies of the human soul.

Oh, Daryl, this will be easy.

"H-hi," he stuttered, playing with his nails.

Daryl's hands were a spectacle, his fingers long and graceful, the kind that would look fitting on a piano or tracing the contours of a lover's back. They were trembling as they played with his immaculately manicured fingernails. His Adam's apple was practically in a cha-cha slide, bobbing up and down as he attempted to maintain some semblance of composure.

"Hey, Love," I winked, cocking my hip against the doorframe like I'd been doing it for years—which, let's face it, I had. "What's your stage name?"

"D-Daryl," he barely managed, eye contact proving to be his Everest.

With a sultry swivel, I sauntered over to the minibar, seizing the gin like it was my birthright. "When's your birthdate, Daryl"

"J-January two… nineteen ninety," he replied, his Adam's apple executing a nervous dance.

Of course. The emotional constipation of a Capricorn merged with Pisces' infuriating over-romanticization of love.

"Hm. Capricorn. Pisces moon." I smirked, my eyes landing on a shiny pearl necklace resting on the side table. Those big. Juicy. Expensive pearls.

My mind couldn't help but drift, carried away on a luxurious daydream. I envisioned myself donning the luminous strands, each pearl a miniature moon glowing against my skin. In my fantasy, they transformed me, elevating me from the smoky backrooms and dim corridors to a life of champagne and chandeliers. The heavy curtain of this underworld would lift, if only for a moment, replaced by the intoxicating aroma of affluence.

The sensation was so palpable, so vivid that for a split second, I lost myself in the illusion. Ah, the beautiful treachery of pearls; they promised an aristocracy of the spirit, a brief escape from the shackles of reality. And oh, how inviting that fantasy was.

I turned back to Daryl, my hand brushing lightly over the pearls. "You like gin, Daryl?"

He nodded, as my own gaze flitted between the necklace and him.

Those pearls weren't just jewelry; they were a ticket, a momentary passport to a dream suspended just beyond my reach. A dream that, for a cunning fox like me, was one step closer to becoming real. And all it took was a little manipulation—my forte, my craft, my ultimate claim to fame.

A look of uncertainty flashed in his eyes, but I was too caught up in my own agenda to notice. "What else do you like, Hun?" I asked, climbing onto the bed, drinks in hand.

"Y-you're very straightforward," he stammered, a blush creeping over his face.

I leaned closer, a coy smile playing on my lips. "Some say that's my best asset."

But in a moment, the air shifted. Panic took over and he was on his feet, heading towards the door. "I can't do this!" he mumbled, and dashed for the door.

The adrenaline surged. I'd been close—so close—to snagging those pearls.

Think, Vixen, think!

"This isn't for me," he admitted, pulling his jacket on.

My brain went into overdrive, as I tried to catch my breath, feeling my heart's rhythm splinter. Angel's cryptic words echoed menacingly. What if this was a setup? My reputation, my safety, everything was on the line. Bambi... I had to do this for Bambi.

My eyes darted around the room. The neon lights, the luxurious velvet drapes, the vintage settee—it all felt suffocating. I caught sight of my reflection, wild-eyed and desperate, in the ornate mirror hanging crookedly on the wall. This wasn't me. I was Vixen, the master of my fate, the commander of my universe. I could manipulate the scenario, flip the table to my advantage. The elements were all here: a vulnerable client, my undeniable charm.

Just when a wild idea popped up—

"Daryl, wait," I lured him back with honeyed words and a swift reach for—my tarot cards.

Although tarot was a tool I often used, my primary guide was always my uncanny ability to tap into people's emotions. "Let's play a little game."

"I don't believe in…" he began, but I cut him off by dramatically drawing the **Two of Cups**. The card of intertwined lovers.

"Lovers. Why are you here, Daryl?" I leaned in, locking eyes.

"I don't know. I thought I wanted to—"

"You do… just not with me," I cut him off, pulling **The Fool** card next—its imagery of a wayward youth potent and direct. Lost. Wandering. "He wanted an open relationship." I quickly followed with the **Three of Swords**, a graphic tri-stab to the heart. "But you, did not." I looked up to Daryl, "Right?"

The change was miraculous. His bewildered eyes turned into saucers of shock. "H-how does anyone know what they really want."

Gotcha.

I sighed, pushing my agenda. "How about you tell me everything about him. I'm all ears."

He looked taken aback, but a small smile formed on his lips. "R-Really?"

I leaned back against the dresser, the pearls pressing cold against my palm. "I'm not really a great listener, but I can make an exception," I squeezed the pearls. "And the best part, it never has to leave this room, Hun," I reassured him, pocketing the necklace.

His grateful smile was my standing ovation. Curtains closed, end scene. I shuffled my tarot deck, smirking triumphantly. The pearls weighed sweetly in my pocket like the ultimate badge of manipulative honour.

You never stood a chance Daryl.

♡ BUBBLE GUM BITCH. ♡

"You really want that street trash here?"

Jacqueline's dance floor pulsed with the energy of a thousand frenzied beats. Colours flashed across the gyrating bodies, the air thick with sweat, desperation, and a hint of cheap straight boy cologne.

Pearls—those delicious trophies from my earlier escapade—caressed my neck as I pranced through this hedonistic crowd, a fistful of twenties clenched in triumph. And there, marinating in her contemplative funk at the bar, was Angel, her black stiletto nail absentmindedly rapping against a champagne flute, next to Emma Royd. Her makeup was smudged, her dress clung to her like second skin, but it was the martini in her hand that commanded attention.

Eavesdropping. My favourite sport.

"How's the new boy-toy?" she asked, an obnoxious grin on her lips, creasing her neck folds. "Didn't scare him off yet, did ya?"

"You needed a replacement for Crystal—" she laughed, "He's not it, Mama," Angel grumbled, snapping at Aspen to pour her another glass. Her eyes flashed like warning lights. "He's so fucking annoying. Delusional. AND—" she tanked her prosecco, "a total narcissist."

Sly Emma took a drag of her cigarette and let out a mocking chuckle. "Big words don't suit you, Sugar."

Angel snapped at Aspen, again. "You really want that street trash here? With us?!"

Emma just laughed, the sound fusing to the music.

Angel wasn't about to back down. "He doesn't know a single thing about escorting—"

Alright that's enough, Bitch.

"Voilà!" My voice cut through their conversation like a knife. I swaggered over, a triumphant grin on my face, and slammed a pile of twenties on the counter. "Oh—wait!" I exclaimed, glaring into Angel's eyes, as I slammed two more piles of twenties in front of her. "Lucky me found a few more clients."

Aspen, wide eyed, grazed the cash with the tip of his fingers, "How much did you make?"

"Roughly a grand," I gloated, my eyes burning into Angel's. "And all I had to do was chat with the lovely fellas. No lewd stuff."

The atmosphere thickened like coagulating blood; my joyously insolent grin was a burning brand. As Angel popped her bubble of gum. I went on. "But that's nothing new for this… street trash." I tossed a stack of twenties at Emma. "Here's your cut Mama."

Bubble gum pop!

My eyes flickered back to Angel as I revelled in the pulsing spotlight. She was grinding her teeth, and for the first time, I noticed the pink wad of bubble gum shifting from one cheek to the other in her mouth. Bubble gum, her talisman; a sugary amulet she'd knead between her molars before launching any sort of attack, verbal or otherwise. It was her ritualistic dance before the pounce, the way a cobra might hiss and sway before striking.

The rhythmic chomping intensified, the sticky mass bulging out as if it were collecting her ire. It was a tell—

like a shark's fin slicing through water—that heralded impending drama. A prelude to her primal roar, her venomous lunge.

Bubble gum pop!

The sound detonated through the atmosphere, an audible snap that broke through even the thumping bass of the music. It was an alarm bell in a wilderness teeming with predators and prey, a challenge in a court where fangs and claws were replaced with snide remarks and cutting glances.

My eyes narrowed. The pink bubble had burst, and with it, any veneer of civilized pretence. The animalistic rites were complete; the enraged beast was ready to leap, to sink her fangs into the flesh of her adversaries.

I smiled, the corners of my mouth stretching wider than ever, thrilled by the promise of the skirmish to come. The dance floor was our arena.

Would she spring? Would she snarl? Either way, Angel's gum-pop had set the stage, and I was more than ready for whatever ferocious performance she was about to unleash.

Bring it on, Angel.

"If you'll excuse me…" With a flourish, I plucked Angel's glass from her grip. "I think I've earned a little twirling around." And I downed her prosecco.

Angel watched as I swallowed a pink pill with her drink and then made my way to the pole, a swagger in my step. And a little snarky wink. I could feel the heat rising in her face, her fingers clenching around her empty flute.

Foot tapping. My knuckles cracking. *Bubble gum pop!*

My mind spun a wild fantasy. I could feel myself in her head. Angel spinning me around, spitting her gum onto my face. Yanking my pearl necklace off, sending each bit flying. And lunging at me. Falling to the ground. Punching the shit out of me. As blood gushes out of my mouth. My blood staining the dance floor, the pearl necklace scattering, a testament to my defeat.

But reality is a cruel mistress.

Bubble gum pop!

I snapped back into reality, Emma's voice cutting through my violent daydream, turned to Angel, "Sugar, I'd focus on your own success if I were you, cause—"

She held up the wad of cash, her eyes wide in astonishment, "This little fox will do just fine."

Angel shot me a glare. If looks could kill, I would be writhing on the floor, bathing in a pool of glitter infused blood.

But instead, I was the tempest at the pole, twirling, unfurling, stretching to the heavens as bills found their way into my thong. Dropping from my aerial pirouette, I blew a mocking kiss Angel's way. I could almost hear her thinking: "The challenge was laid, and I'd be damned if I'd let him win."

♡ TEXTS. TENSIONS. ♡ AND THONGS.

"I'll have the money in no time at all"

My loft really was my sanctuary—a place where the orange hues of the sunset streamed in, introducing the night. A soft breeze danced through, carrying with it the scent of the city and playing with the red rhinestone thong I'd draped over the windowsill the night before to dry. A perfect moment of serenity, ruined by…

Me.

I was lost in the process of painting my nails a deep, glossy black, when my phone came alive with the worried face of Bambi. It was a FaceTime call.

"HELLO?! Babe, can you focus?! I'm not messing around here," Bambi's voice pierced through my momentary calm.

I grabbed the phone, lined my eyes up with Bambi's, and flashed a grin.

Bambi narrowed his eyes, pissed. "What the HELL is up with the money?"

I took a drag from my cigarette, letting the smoke swirl around me before answering. "I got it all figured out," I replied nonchalantly, playing with the pearl necklace.

Bambi squinted, the embers of distrust still glowing in his eyes. "Good. You got that server job?"

"Yep… I'll have the money in—" I hesitated, that familiar anxiety tightening my chest, "no time at all."

Bambi's eyes pierced into mine through the screen. "Okay. Cause Jay's not fucking around…"

Ping!

Ugh… PrideMate again. I glanced at the screen, my heart skipping a beat.

(Quinn): **So, you ready for that date?**

Hiding a smirk, I rolled my eyes, finding myself getting lost in Quinn's message.

"I know you two had a strong bond," Bambi went on, his voice echoing in the distance, "but that's gone, Vix. All the money he stole from you. The harassment…"Between Bambi's nattering and the flicker of my phone screen, my thoughts pirouetted in a chaotic ballet. Quinn's text stared back at me—blinking innocuously on my phone. **"So, you ready for that date?,"** it read.

Was I?

My thumb hovered over the screen, indecisive and trembling.

Should I? I think I want to.

For a moment, I hesitated.

Quinn was a mystery, a riddle wrapped in an enigma, packaged in heart-stopping smiles and magnetic charm. The pull was intoxicating but also, potentially, very dangerous. I was no stranger to dangerous liaisons, but with Jay still breathing down my neck and money troubles crawling like spiders in my mind, was this the best idea?

I blinked, my own reflection gleaming back at me from the black mirror of the phone. Then the words of an old song came into my head—something about shooting for the moon and landing among the stars. Was it cheesy? Hell yes. But did it hold a sliver of truth? Absolutely.

The air thickened as I held my breath, my thumb finally descending like a guillotine. I hit reply.

(Me): **Sure. I'll be over in ten.**

Then pressed send. And there it was, sealed like a kiss or a contract, pulling me further into the whirling vortex.

"Vixen?… who are you texting?" Bambi's voice grew more insistent. Three dots danced on the screen, holding me in suspense. I couldn't look away.

"Earth to Vixen—", Bambi added, concerned.

Ping!

(Quinn): **I have a better spot.**

Twirling the phone back to my face, I winked at Bambi. "No Jay. Get the money. No sweat. Gotta go, Love! Duty calls!" With that, I blew a theatrical kiss to the screen.

"Wait, no! Vix—"

With a flourish, I hung up and reached for my red rhinestone thong.

Who knows? It might come in handy.

♡ STARCHEWS, SMIRKS, ♡ & SUBURBAN FAIRYTALES.

"Tell me something you love"

The night was alive, tinged with the delightful aroma of food from the most god-awful looking food trucks, laughter from insufferably happy couples, and soft fairy lights…

Can't hate on those. Those are cute.

The marketplace seemed to stretch ahead of us for miles, a smorgasbord of tastes waiting to be sampled. Quinn, with his quirky charm, was right at home amidst the gastronomical tapestry, happily munching away on what he called 'artisanal popcorn'.

With a skeptical tilt of my head and a sly grin, I popped a StarChew into my mouth. "Interesting choice."

His eyes twinkled with that damned irresistible mischief. "What do you mean?! Food markets are insane! This is the best of the culinary underworld."

I rolled my eyes dramatically, gesturing around us, "It's your hour, Hun."

He laughed—a sound so warm it could melt glaciers—and passed me some popcorn. Our fingers brushed in the exchange. I felt a flicker of something, some inexplicable tingle, but hastily reverted to my tried-and-true diversion tactics. "So, when's your birth—"

With a mischievous twinkle, he steered the conversation, "I'm a Gemini. With a Leo rising and... an Aquarius moon?"

Of course. It made sense—a little too much sense, actually. The man oozed the duality of a Gemini: gregarious yet thoughtful, intellectual yet playful. It's like he was born to talk, to charm, to hold court in a room full of dazzled subjects. And the Leo rising? That splash of charisma, confidence, and natural leadership? It didn't just make him noticeable; it made him magnetic.

Then there was his Aquarius moon, the quirky cherry on top of his astrological sundae. A flair for the unconventional, an air of unpredictability, and a tendency toward free-spiritedness. This guy wasn't just a puzzle; he was a damn Rubik's Cube.

I smirked as he proudly declared, "Which basically means I have big golden retriever energy. Can't shut up. And love to give a show!" He grinned unabashedly, adding a casual "or so I was told."

He had boiled down his complex astrological chart into a cutesy one-liner, but he'd hit the nail on the head.

The laughter was barely out of my mouth when my phone dinged, jarring my nerves.

(The Devil): **Tick Tock. Doll.**

I nervously chewed at the black polish on my nails. He noticed, of course. Quinn's eyes were ever watchful, curious. "What about you? Tell me something," he pressed, determined to peel away my layers.

There's no way.

"Yeah—I understand nothing of astrology so… maybe your… backstory?" Quinn added.

Even worse.

"I'm whoever you want me to be," I flirted, dodging the question, "That's kind of the point," I winked. "What's yours?"

"Nothing too exciting. Typical suburban childhood. Great mom and dad. Annoying little sister."

I couldn't help but smile for some reason.

He went on. "We were very family-oriented. We'd always spend our summers at some cottage deep in the forest… kayaking. Eating way too many s'mores by the fire—You know… classic nature freak stuff," he slipped a smile, lost in his pleasant memories, "My folks helped me start up my Airbnb rentals and—yeah…" He raised his shoulders, finishing off with a wistful, "pretty simple life," his gaze softening as he took in my reaction.

Pretty simple life.

My mind began to wander into unfamiliar territory, caught in the gravitational pull of his narrative. A childhood so wholesome it could be a vintage postcard. Picture-perfect summers, an irritating little sister who's probably cute as hell, loving parents, and a life cushioned by the mundane but heartfelt joys of suburban existence. It was the kind of family you'd expect to find on the cover of a brochure about America, where everyone wears matching sweaters and smiles as though they've never known a day of sorrow.

The sheer simplicity of it was like hearing a fairy tale from some parallel universe—bewitching, but completely foreign. What would it be like, I wondered, to grow up in a world where your biggest concern was losing a paddle during a kayaking trip? Where the evening bonfires glowed brighter than neon signs of a nightclub, and the air was thick with the scent of toasted marshmallows rather than stale cigarettes and fading perfume?

I shook my head as if to dispel the daydream, suddenly aware of a pang of something I couldn't quite place—envy, longing, a bittersweet nostalgia for a life never lived. The sensation was disorienting.

For a fleeting moment, I glimpsed a world so drastically different from mine yet so touchingly beautiful in its mundane perfection. But all I could murmur was a faint, "must've been nice…" as I looked away.

Trying to lighten the mood, Quinn changed the subject. "Tell me something you love! That's kinda weird, but you just LOVE it. And no one knows."

I was about to dodge again. "I don't give out personal deets on the job—"

"I'll start," he said, with his stupid little smirk.

God I hate that smirk.

Quinn cleared his throat, in preparation of his monologue. "I… am quite terrible at Rock Paper Scissors. It's pretty bad actually. That game is out to get me," he laughed, "I believe green to be the superior colour. We can debate later. I'll most likely win though," he smiled, "I have this slightly alarming wheeze whenever I laugh. And yes. Got it checked out so please…" he slipped the least cocky wink I had ever seen, "No need to panic— AND I'm part of the celery with peanut butter fan club."

Grimacing, I shook my head, "that's disgusting…"

"Hey—it's delicious and even better with dates!" he insisted, nudging me playfully.

I swiftly gagged. As he went on. His chuckle was warm. "Try it first. Then come back to me. You'll see," he paused for a bit, staring into my eyes, as if he was trying to peel every layer apart, "your turn."

Under his persistent gaze, my defences weakened. "Astrology, tarot, and—Old Hollywood movies," I confessed.

His response was teasing, "Old Hollywood movies?"

"Yeah, fucking Old Hollywood movies. What's wrong with that?!" My cheeks burned, and I suddenly felt like I'd ripped a page out of my journal and handed it to him on a silver platter. It wasn't like me to share anything truly personal, especially not my love for the glamour and faux simplicity of a bygone era.

He played innocent, "No—no, nothing. Please, go on."

I hesitated, warring between my impulse to protect the sanctuary of my inner life and the strange, disquieting desire to let someone else in. Finally, I took the plunge, pulling out another StarChew, "I love those films. You know like, Hello Dolly… with Barbra Streisand. Everyone's just… always refined. And rich. And they're all just so… happy."

What the fuck am I doing.

I quickly snapped back to reality, "It just feels nice to watch."

Why had I said it? Sure, astrology and tarot were easy to share, part of my known persona. But Old Hollywood films? That was sacred ground, a private oasis where I retreated when life became too chaotic even for me. Where the men wore tuxedos, and the women floated in dresses that dripped with pearls and sequins. It was a world where dialogue snapped and sizzled, where lovers danced in ballrooms that glittered like the night sky, where for an hour or two, I could imagine I was someone else entirely—someone graceful, understood, and indescribably elegant.

But here I was, that guarded secret now dangling in the air between us like the string of pearls around my neck. Vulnerable.

"That is… quite a lot of personal 'deets' right there, Vixen," he mused with a smirk, as I smiled, fiddling like a dumb idiot with my pearl necklace. "Way to break your own rules—"Just as his phone beeped.

"Would you look at that. My hour's up," he observed, still smiling. "You're not really good at keeping tabs on your clients, are you?"

I chuckled at his joke, as he added, "How about I book you for another hour sometime."

I rolled my eyes, trying to play it cool. "We'll see—" I drawled.

But Quinn, ever the spontaneous Gemini, had another idea. "What about now? You've got your Sunday clothes on. Why don't I take you on an adventure, Dolly," he smirked.

That inescapable, endearing, damn smirk…

I was snared, lured into Quinn's peculiar orbit, destined for... well, who knew? And as the great Carrie Bradshaw would probably say:

And just like that, with a sly grin, some quirky golden retriever and a cherry StarChew, I found myself being pulled into Quinn's whirlwind.

Whereas I would have probably just said:

I'm royally fucked.

♡ STRANGERS ♡ IN THE NIGHT.

"Dance with me"

Lasers cut through the thick, foggy air, of Suite 701. The kind of club with fully naked go-go dancers, but it was still somehow giving class. Vibrant neon lights danced on and off the walls, as the pulsating beats shook the very foundation. Throbbing in time with my erratic heart.

Quinn materialized next to me, pulling me out of my strobe-light reverie. "More your vibe?" he crooned, voice dripping with that sort of Gemini charm you can't help but eat up. One of those smiles that could coax angels into sin flickered across his lips. He winked.

Quinn had that kind of magnetism that turned heads the moment he walked into a room—but don't mistake it for mere flash; it was a slow-burning charisma, one that simmered and deepened the longer you knew him. Standing tall, he carried himself with a relaxed self-assuredness that was far removed from cockiness. It wasn't an arrogant strut but a composed saunter, as though he knew exactly where he was going and invited you to follow, if you dared.

The thrum of techno drowned our voices, but our eyes communicated just fine. At the bar, Quinn took charge, "Two gin—" He turned to me, "You like gin? You look like a gin guy?"

I nodded with approval.

He was everything I loved to hate. Suave but not slick, attention-grabbing but never attention-seeking. Think Gatsby but without the overwrought tragic backstory— just a guy who floated through life making everyone feel a little more enchanted. A confident stroll, not a pompous stride; the difference between an Instagram filter and the real thing.

"Two gin tonics!" he shouted over to the bartender, turning back to me, "Extra lime on one. That cool?"

For all my well-maintained façade of being unfazed and ever-ready for whatever the universe threw at me, I felt a tremor of unfamiliar nerves. Maybe it was his unyielding gaze or the fact that, despite myself, I was genuinely captivated.

My hand surreptitiously slid toward my pocket, seeking the powdered security blanket I'd smuggled in—a tiny bag of premium-grade MDMA.

And just as my fingertips grazed the crinkled plastic, almost as if summoned by some cosmic joke or a fluke alignment of stars, Quinn turned back with drinks in hand and thrust a gin tonic towards me. "Here. Cheers!" he announced.

I looked at him, then at the drink, and couldn't help but think that maybe, just maybe, the universe was telling me something.

We clinked glasses, and that undercurrent of tension turned into a full-blown electric charge, buzzing from the lime wedge all the way to my jittery, disarmed soul.

I gulped down my entire drink, Quinn teased, "Or that!" He laughed and looked me deep in the eyes, whispering, "dance with me."

He pulled me toward the dance floor, the gravitational pull between us more magnetic than ever. We were two souls lost in the hypnotic rhythm, dancing the night away.

Faintly brushing each other's hands. Clumsily looking into one another's eyes. Dancing the night away.

The words he whispered seemed to hang in the air, even as we spun and swayed to the thumping beats.

Dance with me.

Soft. Understated. A request wrapped in a velvet promise that contrasted sharply with the blaring synths and crashing cymbals around us. It wasn't shouted over the music, but rather, it slipped into a silent pocket of space just long enough for those three words to imprint themselves indelibly on my mind.

And the way he said it—like he was sharing a secret, handing me a key to some hidden room inside him—that vulnerability coated the syllables, turning them into something almost sacred. I could feel my insides churn, a swirl of anticipation and nerves that even the MDMA, had I taken it, couldn't have produced.

This wasn't a casual invitation. It wasn't a question. It was a line that could haunt you for the rest of your life— becoming a ghost of a moment, replaying in the depths of 3 a.m. thoughts, reminding you of that one time, in that one place, when someone asked you to be completely present, even if just for a song.

Dance with me.

And as we lost ourselves in the rhythm, the electricity between us palpable, those words took on a life of their own, becoming a mantra that could pull me back to this moment, to Quinn, over and over again. For the rest of my life. Just when—

Pulling out a pair of AirPods, Quinn waved them in front of me, and despite the setting, I couldn't help but chuckle, "Really?" I had to stop my eyes from rolling.

His playful tone retorted, "Hey! I paid for this hour!" He winked, "Humour me!"

I smiled, tossing my empty glass into some drunk's hoodie hood. I slipped the AirPods in, and suddenly Sinatra's "Strangers in the Night" crooning filled my ears, contrasting starkly with the pounding techno that still vibrated through the floor beneath us. The contrast was jarring but inexplicably perfect. Our worlds zoned into just the two of us.

Sinatra, the epitome of Old Hollywood class, in this den of modern excess—it was discordant and yet, it felt strangely right. And that's when it hit me: the tackiness didn't matter. In that moment, it was as if Quinn had cleared away all the noise, and there was only us.

There was something comforting about his gaze—deep, and unwavering. The joy on his face mirrored in my eyes, the weight of my past temporarily lifted. I could feel my wince turning into a soft smile. For a moment, I forgot my crafted persona, my curated life of tarot and astrology, of Old Hollywood movies and a veneer of chaotic mysticism.

As "Strangers in the Night" softly played, its lyrics ironically apt for our current situation, I felt like the protagonist in some romantic movie scene I'd watched a thousand times but never thought I'd experience. The universe was laughing at me, or maybe it was nudging me toward something more authentic than any reading of tarot cards or astrology charts could ever offer.

The moment elongated, stretching into something too precious to disturb with words. As we swayed to the soft rhythms of Sinatra, I realized my tried-and-true diversion tactics were failing me. I was falling, falling for Quinn's genuine attentiveness, his warmth, his words. And as much as I struggled to shove those blooming feelings back into some dark corner of my psyche, they continued to spill over, filling me up until I thought I might burst.

So we danced. Two strangers in the night. And though Sinatra's voice whispered tales of fleeting love, for the first time, I started to consider the possibility that some encounters—some dances—were worth lingering over, long after the music stopped.

When suddenly, he reached for my neck and—

WHAM!

I slapped him. A reflex, hardwired from too many dark memories. "FUCK! SORRY. It's a reflex…" I winced.

He laughed, trying to lighten the mood, "Noted."

But the universe had other plans. A jolt in the crowd shoved him into me, breaking all pretences of personal space. Our bodies meshed together, awfully close, his breath a hot whisper against my face. The moment stretched taut between us, pulled to the point of snapping.

He tilted up my chin and the world froze, crystallized into a singular, electric instant. My heart racing. And then his lips met mine—a soft, perfectly imprecise kiss that shattered and remade my universe in the time it takes for a beat to drop.

A soft, gentle kiss, from this quirky, ever-so-annoying, stranger in the night.

♡ PROPHECY. ♡

"So is this another paid hour, or?"

We burst into Quinn's bedroom, an all-consuming urgency in our steps, only to be thwarted by a rogue pair of cowboy boots, of all things. Quinn tripped, but we both laughed it off. It was like a pratfall straight out of some rom-com, and I loved it.

The ambiance of his room struck me almost immediately: moonlight spilled onto an old cowboy hat, and the plaid flannel sheets on the log-frame bed emitted an inviting coziness. A cottage-core-Brokeback-Mountain cross-over.

Raising an eyebrow, I remarked, "A lumberjack cowboy. That's a first."

Quinn, amused by my observation, played along, "What?! The great Vixen has never re-enacted an indoor

Brokeback Mountain fantasy?!" He tilted my chin up to meet his eyes, a portal to someplace warm and infinite, "Shocking."

His close proximity made me shiver, and the spark in his eyes even more so. His features were a study in balanced contrast: there was a rugged appeal to him, but it was softened, made infinitely more interesting by hints of kindness and a sense of depth. Thick, well-defined eyebrows served as a natural frame for expressive eyes that looked like they were guarding centuries of old-world wisdom or perhaps modern secrets. When he fixed those eyes on you, it was enough to make you feel like the only person in a crowded room.

But it was his smile that was the true showstopper.

That fucking smile.

It started as a small curling at the corners of his lips, a little prelude to the symphony. And when it unfurled fully, it was dazzling, incandescent, like a lighthouse guiding ships safely through the stormiest seas. You found yourself thinking that smile could end wars, mend hearts, or at the very least, brighten the gloomiest of days.

The space between us was electric, crackling with the tension of a brewing storm. For a moment, Quinn and I were caught in a suspended reality. Then, in a surge of movement that could rival any force of nature, our lips crashed together.

It was as if we were trying to consume the energy that swirled around us, to taste the intoxicating blend of gin, lime, and something far more primal. The feel of his lips, soft yet insistent, pulled me further into the vortex of desire that had been building since the moment our eyes met in that dimly lit corridor.

His hands found their way to the small of my back, urging me closer until our bodies were flush against each other. I responded in kind, my own hands threading through his hair, tugging gently in a rhythm that elicited a low growl from the back of his throat.

With an almost animalistic urgency, we made our way towards the bed, shedding layers of clothing like a snake moulting its skin. The bed seemed miles away, but finally, we toppled onto it. He hovered over me, his eyes searching mine as if looking for permission. What he saw must have satisfied him because the corners of his lips curled into that maddening, irresistible smile.

"That smile is going to get you into trouble one of these days," I said, voice tinged with playful threat and promise.

"I'm counting on it," he replied, before capturing my lips once more.

As his mouth explored the contours of my neck, sending tingles of pleasure down my spine, his hand brushed against something hard in my pocket. He paused, his eyes sparkling with curiosity and perhaps a hint of mischief.

"What's this? Happy to see me?" he asked, fishing out my tarot deck from the pocket of my discarded jeans.

The abrupt change in the atmosphere was palpable, but rather than making it awkward, the tarot cards added an extra layer of mystery, a bit of that chaotic magic that seemed to define me.

"Burn the witch!" he exclaimed jokingly.

The laughter that bubbled up from within me felt almost cathartic, a release of tension that only heightened the emotional intimacy of the moment.

"You have no idea," I said, placing the tarot deck on the nightstand, as though tucking away a ticking time bomb. But Quinn wasn't one to let mysteries lie dormant.

"Read me," he insisted, his voice a husky whisper.

I gave him a look that I hoped was both enigmatic and teasing. "I think there are more important things to do right now."

But the cards, once brought into the spotlight, seemed to radiate an aura of impending revelations. It was as if they were screaming to spill their secrets, to dance in the chaos that always wove itself around me.

As we surrendered once more to the tactile and tantalizingly immediate, they sat silently on the nightstand, their secrets sealed for the moment, overshadowed by the more immediate, more tangible mysteries unfolding between Quinn and I.

Still wrapped in the tangled cocoon of bedsheets, our breaths began to steady. The room was thick with a combination of sweat, pheromones, and that indescribable electric charge that follows a moment of intense closeness. Quinn looked over at me, his gaze softer but still tinged with that insatiable curiosity.

"You know, you still owe me that tarot reading," he said, his voice imbued with a post-intimate glow.

I chuckled. "Ah, right. Because the best moment for a deeply spiritual divination is right after—"

"Hey, the divine doesn't wait for anyone," he winked, reaching for the tarot deck on the nightstand.

"Right," I conceded, feeling both excited and a bit nervous about peering into the potential futures of this complex man lying beside me.

Shuffling the cards with a concentrated face, I could feel Quinn's eyes on me, watching every movement with fascination. It was as if they were seeking a magic trick in a deck that promised only truths—some beautiful, some unsettling.

A part of me was apprehensive. Tarot readings were intimate and often revealed the deepest shadows of one's heart and past. While predicting some form of ambiguously twisted future… but, looking into Quinn's eager eyes, I complied.

"Don't be upset if you don't like what it says," I said in my staple mysterious charm.

I placed three cards face down and flipped the first one, "Past…"

The first card: **The Devil**. A chill ran down my spine as the menacing horned figure stared back. A familiar sight.

I flipped the second, "Present…"

The second card: **The Lovers**. The illustration of two figures in a passionate embrace made my cheeks flush with a shade of pink.

I flipped the third, "Future—"

Death. The weight of its meaning hung heavily between us. Quinn, inquisitive, turned to me, "What does it mean?"

I chose to deflect, unsure of the exact game the divine Spirits were teasing me with…

It can mean a million things.

Death: the most misunderstood, the most feared, yet one of the most transformative cards in the tarot deck. It could signify endings, but also new beginnings; it could be a transformation, a radical change, the death of an old way to make room for something new. Hell, sometimes it even meant literal death.

Was it signalling the end of my solitary ways? A rebirth into something... more? Or was it hinting at the temporary nature of our passion, the fiery but quick-burning flare of a relationship destined to become ash? My head swirled with possibilities, each as likely and as unlikely as the next. It was like trying to read the end of a choose-your-own-adventure book by starting from the middle.

And that's what threw me: I, who had always felt so in tune with the unseen, so connected to the world's cosmic whispers, was baffled. I couldn't pinpoint which interpretation resonated in this electric moment with Quinn. His eyes were asking for an explanation, a revelation, something only the cards and I could offer.

But the card remained elusive, dancing around my attempts to pin it down. The many facets of its symbolism sparkled like gems in the moonlight, so numerous that they muddled rather than clarified. Was it a beautiful but fatalistic prophecy, or a warning to be heeded?

I tried to spin the meaning, "An exciting, whirlwind of an adventure awaits…" I looked him up and down, "hopefully one where you'll learn to dress better."

Quinn chuckled, "I dress fine, thank you very much!" He nudged me, "So is this another paid hour, or?…"

I pushed him onto the bed. "Shut up!" I exclaimed, laughing and squeezing him in.

But the restless sorcerer in me needed a clearer answer. As Quinn revelled in our playful tussle, I discreetly drew a fourth card: **The Tower**. The room seemed to dim a shade. A symbol of abrupt upheaval, of chaos and calamity. Heights. Destruction. The crumbling of it all.

The terror it brought me was inexplicable. Although our playful banter continued, in the back of my mind, the looming thought:

Was this some twisted omen?

♡ WHISPERS OF ♡ A STRIPPER.

"See you tomorrow?… maybe?"

In a whirl of sensuality and sonic nostalgia, I spun through my loft—blasting some 60s country classics. The music was like a balm, soothing the storm of emotions inside me.

The room, with its scattered heels and thongs, felt like a messy memory bank, reminders of nights less lonely and mornings less clear. But somehow… I wasn't interested in them. The music worked its magic like liquid tranquility, calming the raging sea within me. Each twang of the guitar, each lyrical whisper was a salve on my restless soul. In between the heart-tugging chords and bittersweet crooning, I paused, absorbing the feeling that only '60s country music could invoke in me.

There was a sense of nostalgia that couldn't quite be placed, like déjà vu in it. Even though I hadn't lived through that decade, every tune was a capsule of emotion, transporting me to a time when the world seemed simpler, yet charged with the nuance of human emotion. It was the voice of yearning, of love lost and found, of pain and triumph; a sonic tapestry woven with threads of honest feelings and experiences.

But it wasn't just the bittersweet melancholy that drew me in. No, there was something more—like each song was an incantation of hope. Those country singers, with their warbly voices and world-weary eyes, seemed to capture an intrinsic optimism. Even in tales of heartbreak and sorrow, there was a glimmer of light, a crack through which the future's brightness could spill. It's as if they were telling me, "Kid, life is a maze of ups and downs, but keep the faith. The ride's worth it."

This music was my anchor. It grounded me, reminding me that every emotion was a piece of art, every moment —good or bad—a lyric in the long-running country song of my life. It was comfort, it was catharsis, it was like a long, soothing hug from a bygone era telling me, "You're going to be okay."

Dressed, or rather undressed, in nothing but my sexy as fuck black panties, I embraced the audacious spirit that always seemed to find its way out during these private moments. I was mid-twirl, the world a blur, when an all-too-familiar sound echoed.

Ping!

The phone's chirp cut through the music, snapping me back into reality. Grabbing my phone—

(Quinn): **What a night, Dolly! See you tomorrow?... maybe?**

That stupid lil' cowboy.

Quinn. Just his name sent a torrent of memories crashing: the night, the dance, the whispers. His cheeky use of 'Dolly' made my lips curve into a smirk. The little hints of our shared banter, the references to old Hollywood films, my secret interests... it felt so pure. So honest.

I cued up another country classic. This genre had become my confessional, my oral history set to the rhythms of steel guitars and smoky vocals.

As I resumed my intimate dance, memories of Quinn enfolded me like a shroud of paradoxical warmth—electric yet comforting. Our interlude at Suite 701, Sinatra serenading us amidst the cacophony of techno beats. That log-cabin bedroom basked in milky moonlight, where the texture of Quinn's skin had blended with the raw elements of wood and air.

What was most captivating was how genuine he appeared. There was no sense of a facade or a rehearsed personality; he seemed to offer the authentic version of himself, take it or leave it. And honestly, once you'd had even a glimpse, leaving it was the last thing on your mind.

And then, there were those tarot cards—cards that hinted at a future both tantalizing and foreboding

Yet above all, it was the card I'd hidden—**The Tower** —that haunted me. That emblem of drastic upheaval and the unpredictable, looming like a pending storm on our horizon. Was the universe setting the stage for tragedy, or just dicking around in its cosmic sandbox?

Ugh, Universe, you're so fucking dramatic.

My mind then wandered to Jay's ominous words, his thinly veiled threats that hung in the air like dark clouds.

Could The Tower be related to that? Was the universe giving me a heads-up that Jay's malign presence would resurge to rattle my newfound tranquility? Was the peace I felt, the connection I had found with Quinn, standing on a precipice of ruin?

Jay had been a storm, yes, but I'd weathered storms before. And Quinn, well, he felt like the eye of the hurricane—calm and serene, but with an exciting edge of unpredictability.

The Tower was a card of upheaval, yes, but also one of necessary change. Maybe, just maybe, it was a sign that I needed to tear down the old to make way for something new. A new chapter, a new love, a new risk?

As the final chords of the song rang through the loft, I stopped, suddenly weighed down by the gravity of introspection. Was I prepared to delve back into the enigmatic narrative that was Quinn? Was I willing to dance with fate, unscripted and unguarded? I took a moment, a tiny pocket of eternity, to consider whether I was really ready for the sequel. They can be disastrous or divine; the trick is, you never know until the credits roll.

Jacqueline's was as packed as ever. With eager hands reaching out, ready to cop a feel, as I gyrated around that all-too-familiar pole as if it were my stage, my confessional, my altar.

I felt an almost electric connection to the music. It flowed through my veins, guiding each fluid motion, each tantalizing tease of the twenties that slipped into my thong. Yet, it was not the club's usual techno… no. The usual hubbub dimmed momentarily in my mind, as Sinatra's Strangers in the Night played from my AirPods, caressing my eardrums. Enveloping the room.

Continuing to reign supreme in my mind, its sultry notes echoing as I embraced the polished steel of the pole. It felt cool, solid, reliable—a contrast to the world that seemed to shift and twirl around me.

Cash—crisp twenties—materialized in the lace confines of my thong. Sinatra and I were making money tonight, though he was probably rolling in his grave. From my vantage point, everything else was a colourful, blurred haze of light and shadow—except for in one corner.

There Angel sat, shrouded in whispers and self-appointed mystery, her eyes piercing through the darkness, targeting me. If eyes could kill, I would've dropped dead mid-twirl, a victim of her unspoken vendetta. Leaning in to share whispered secrets with Kitty and Aspen. Angel, with her darting eyes and hushed tone, appeared to be on a mission.

And by the way her gaze occasionally darted toward me, it was clear I was the subject of her little tête-à-tête.

Yet, for all of Angel's whispered efforts, Kitty seemed unaffected. Her eyes, wide and gleaming with mischief, would drift towards me and then flutter back to Angel, a playful giggle escaping her lips.

Every so often, she'd interrupt Angel with a carefree, "Another bill!" or "He's such a rockstar, isn't he?"

Each of Kitty's ridiculous exclamations burst into the air like fireworks, sputtering out Angel's whispers before they could take form. It was like watching a soap bubble collide with a needle, vanishing in a puff of iridescent mist.

Then there was Aspen, a stoic iceberg in this sea of frenetic emotion. He sipped his drink his face an impassive mask. True to his nature, he offered very little to the conversation.

"He looks chill," he'd comment succinctly whenever his gaze met mine, a statement that seemed to irk Angel even more…

This bitch.

There she was, her eyes so narrowly focused on me that I almost expected laser beams to shoot out of them. Why such intensity? Why such malice?

Angel was no simple read; she was a novel of complexities written in a language only she fully understood. I'd known many like her in my time—those who seem to exude bitterness as effortlessly as they breathe. But this felt personal, and for the life of me, I couldn't fathom why.

Was it a sense of territoriality, as if my very existence threatened her reign over her little kingdom in Jacqueline's corner booth? Was it envy—of what, though? The attention, the applause, the impromptu camaraderie that often erupted around me? Or was it something deeper, darker, a skeleton neither of us could see but only sense in the closet of her soul?

I've seen gazes like hers before—darts wrapped in velvet. They pierce you softly, so it takes you a moment to realize you've been hit. But the poison seeps in slow and stays long.

At that moment, the absurdity of it struck me. Here we were, adults who could have been anywhere else—chasing dreams, falling in love, finding ourselves. Instead, we chose to be in this sultry cavern, playing these midnight games that didn't seem to have any winners.

As Sinatra's voice crescendoed to its climax, I knew it was my time to deliver. I executed a spin that defied gravity and landed as though I were alighting on the moon, graceful and untouchable.

With a flirtatious wink aimed directly at Kitty, whose exuberant clap was almost a punctuation in itself, I let the energy of the room crest into applause.

Angel? She could eat her whispers for dinner, a dish served colder than Aspen's resting bitch face.

It could've been a scene from a high-school drama. But it wasn't. It was Jacqueline's. And that night, in that den of varied reputations and ill-advised decisions, I didn't just rule the pole; I was the king of whispers and the anarchic conductor.

♡ LOVE NOTES ♡
& NIPPLE COVERS.

"Hello, Dolly. See you tonight!"

The dim lighting of the loft, paired with a soft, repetitive hum from the heart-shaped neon sign outside, created a cozy ambiance. Settled on the lush carpet, cash from the night's escapades fanned around me, I began to count my earnings. The subtle, crisp aroma of gin mingled with the scent of success. The cool glass of the drink was a reward as I sipped, reflecting on a night well spent.

But my moment of self-congratulation was interrupted as Quinn sauntered in with a mischievous glint in his eyes and his cowboy hat in hand. Deciding to try his hand—or rather, his body—at the art of pole dancing, he swung around the sleek metal in an exaggerated, clumsy attempt at sensuality. Each quirky movement, the exaggerated pouts, the comic hip thrusts—he was less of a seductive stripper and more of a malfunctioning robot.

That stupid lil' cowboy.

Rolling my eyes with all the drama I could muster—a skill I'd perfected, thank you very much—I nonetheless couldn't look away. It was like watching a train derail but in the most enchanting way possible. Quinn was a mess, but he was my kind of mess. Each misstep, every exaggerated move, made my heart race—whether from irritation or attraction, I refused to acknowledge. Trust Quinn to turn a simple evening into a show.

Pausing my counting, I carefully stashed my cash inside the safe confines of my sparkly disco ball—a relic from a past gig that now served a more practical purpose. As I closed the latch, my gaze returned to the pole, but Quinn was gone.

Then, from the shadows, he emerged—fully nude, save for his cowboy hat he held... strategically.

Damn him. Damn his audacity, his smirk, his every being that unsettled my carefully constructed barriers.

"You think that's supposed to impress me?" I sneered, even though a part of me, a part I fought against, was undeniably stirred.

His smirk deepened. "Oh, I know it does."

Without another word, I reached for him, pulling him onto the cowhide rug. A battle of lips and wills commenced. It wasn't gentle—it was a claiming, a resistance, a dance of two souls who both challenged and completed each other.

Our laughter melted into passion, hearts racing, and the outside world fading. The loft became our world, and for a few hours, nothing else mattered. We were simply Quinn and Vixen—beautifully, free.

Fucking sunlight.

The sun had the nerve to break into my room, casting fragmented patterns across the floor, breaking the illusion, shards of reality filtering in.

God, I hate sunlight.

Stirring from the bed, I felt an emptiness beside me—a space that had been filled with the weight of a human puzzle named Quinn.

My eyes fluttered open to an almost laughable sight. There, wedged into the jagged terrain of my fractured window, a heart-shaped nipple cover—certainly not mine—clung for dear life. Scrawled on it in that hasty handwriting of Quinn's: **Hello, Dolly. See you tonight!**

A conflicted warmth ignited within me, cheeks tinged with pink. The weirdness of the man. But also, the tenderness of it, an intimacy I wasn't ready to accept. Before I could delve deeper, the harsh buzz of my phone shattered the moment.

Glancing at the screen, the familiar coldness seeped in:

(The Devil): **Halfway there.**

The smile that had just bloomed wilted instantly. I hurled the phone onto the bed, where it bounced twice before settling like a petulant child. A sigh clawed its way out of me, dragging a swell of anxiety with it.

Cursing, the turmoil inside me grew—a blend of external pressures and a budding affection I desperately wanted to deny. The world demanded so much of me, but beneath the facade, vulnerabilities hid, and Quinn was dangerously close to unveiling them all.

Really, the nerve of the guy, waltzing into my life and actually making me feel things! For a moment, I wished I could bottle these emotions and hurl them into the abyss.

But, staring at the heart-shaped nipple cover… the ever-so-simple handwriting—**Hello Dolly.**

I simply smiled.

♡ THE WHEEL ♡ OF FORTUNE.

"What goes around, comes around"

The evening had an electric charge. Maybe it was the neon lights. Maybe it was Jacqueline's crowd. Or maybe, it was just me, stepping into my power, as I carried a couple fifty dollar bills in my back pocket, heading straight to my cash-making den.

Another day to slay.

Angel glowered at me from across the dim-lit hallway. Her resentment was palpable, a festering wound. But tonight, I wasn't here for vendettas, real or imagined. A purposeful stride took me straight to Emma Royd. Her eyelids, heavy with glitter, blinked up in surprise as I handed her a thick wad of cash. It was more about the message than the money.

"Keep the change," I smirked, watching her eyes grow wide.

Stew on that, Angel.

Backroom number six was my sanctuary. Draped in velvet, it smelled like incense and rebellion. This was my chapel where I played high priest, dealing out tarot like divine scripture for the nightly pilgrims. And tonight, the congregation was diverse—a bouncer closeted deeper than Narnia, flanked by the enigmatic Aspen and the human sparkle, Kitty.

Aspen, that quiet storm, eyes holding tragedies and secrets like constellations, sat with a spine straighter than he probably wished he could openly be, watching the cards like a hawk. Opposite him, Kitty was a fireworks show in human form, effervescence bottled into a petite frame. Oh, the delicious contradiction of it all—like pairing champagne with a whiskey chaser.

The air swirled with a cocktail of every vice imaginable—money, temptation, a sprinkle of taboo—all punctuated by the room's laughter and kinetic energy. Kitty tossed cash into the air, a monsoon of green fluttering down upon us. Aspen nodded in tacit approval, as though stamping each bill with his personal seal of 'Yeah, that's cool.'

During the reading, when the **Wheel of Fortune** appeared with a flourish, my eyes darted to the bouncer's outstretched hand. There, gleaming under the dim lighting, was a magnificent ring—a jewel that screamed power and influence. A dangerous desire welled up within me.

Don't mind if I do.

I lifted the card, exposing its vivid imagery to the small congregation.

"The Wheel of Fortune," I intoned, my voice dropping to a velvety timbre reminiscent of the transatlantic accent. "Life's a trip, isn't it? One minute you're on top, next you're at the bottom of the barrel. That's karma for ya—what goes around, comes around."

The words dripped irony so thick you could slice it, as my eyes met the bouncer's. He was entranced, bewitched by the web of my words and the magnetic allure I laid on thicker than my eyeliner.

Misdirection is an art form, Hun.

"But," I continued, drawing nearer to him and letting my hand rest on his, "sometimes you gotta fuck the system, right? Grab that wheel and spin it yourself."

My fingers gently caressed his hand, then slid up his arm, making a stealthy move toward the ostentatious ring that clung to him like an overeager groupie. As I spoke the next words, my fingers, now seasoned magicians, performed their sly trick, rolling the ring off his finger and into my palm with a skill that would put Houdini to shame.

"Cuz let's be real, no one's going to hand you your destiny on a silver platter, Hun. It's not just about riding the wheel; it's about knowing when to jump off, to defy cosmic rules, to seize your own destiny," I concluded, pulling away, the ring now hidden in a secret pocket.

The bouncer blinked, snapping out of the enchantment. He was none the wiser, thoroughly convinced that the card and my allure had offered him some sort of life-changing revelation. In a way, it had, though... he just wouldn't realize it until later.

As I stood back, concluding the ceremony of insight and mystique, the irony wasn't lost on me. But hey, one man's fortune is another man's luck, and tonight, the wheel just spun in my favour.

I was both director and star. Vixen, the unpredictable orchestrator of fate, had pulled off another dazzling caper. And let me tell you, tonight, every card in the deck was a joker. Just when—

Kitty's embrace enveloped me, her euphoria contagious. "Vixen, you're like a psychic rock star!" Aspen's eyes twinkled with an approving gleam—a rarity worth more than the ring nestling in my pocket.

As they prepared to leave the room, a curious sensation washed over me, not unlike a ripple in a pond whose stone's origin you can't quite place. Kitty enveloped me in a hug—genuine, unguarded—her eyes twinkling as if we shared a secret. Aspen, normally so reserved, graced me with a nod and a subtle smirk that spoke volumes. The air hung heavy for a moment, and I realized something that was quite alienating to me.

They like me.

For a split second, I stood there, stunned. The room felt oddly empty when they left, as if they took a bit of its soul with them—a soul I didn't even know existed until just now. It was a perplexing, almost unnerving moment of clarity. I was accustomed to webs of manipulation, to a life where every interaction was a calculated move. But this? This felt like something you couldn't put a price on.

Emotional bonds were messy, unnecessary—liabilities. But this unspoken connection with Kitty and Aspen left me questioning those long-standing beliefs.

Could I, a master of illusion and disguise, belong somewhere so authentically?

I shook my head, refocusing on the task at hand. I tucked the newly acquired ring into its velvet sanctuary, but as I did, a pang of something akin to guilt struck me. No, not guilt—uncertainty. As if I'd won a game but wasn't entirely sure of the prize.

♡ SINGIN' IN ♡ THE RAIN.

"God you're weird"

Elegantly plucking a stack of hundred-dollar bills, I sauntered toward the relic that held my reserves—my glitzy disco ball. As I nestled the cash into the sphere's hollow core, securing it with a meticulous twist, the doorbell rang—insistent—demanding, unapologetic. Swinging the door open, there he stood.

Quinn, in all his infuriating splendour, eyes gleaming with mischief and a hint of excitement. And as if answering a question I never asked, he hoisted up two retina-searing yellow ponchos. My eyebrows vaulted skyward, a silent sentinel of my skepticism. Another one of Quinn's eccentric plans, no doubt.

Before I could form a question, my phone interrupted with its familiar—

Ping!

(Quinn): **Did you like 'Singing in the rain'?**

That showman. That incorrigible, audacious showman. Because who else would text me from literally three feet away?

Damn him and his theatrics.

The heavens ruptured like an overwrought dam, dousing the city in an aqueous spectacle. Rain lashed in torrents, shrouding the world in a cloak of liquid grey. Our absurdly yellow ponchos were the only interruption. We resembled radioactive ducklings in an industrial wasteland, and it was sublimely ridiculous.

Quinn didn't hesitate. He was in his element. With gleeful eyes that outshone our synthetic plumage, he thrust one of his AirPods into my hands and swept me into the aquatic theatre beyond the doorstep. Cars whooshed past, spraying arcs of water, their horns trumpeting like disoriented elephants in a rainforest—were they vexed or vicariously thrilled? It didn't matter.

With the grace of a man unshackled from societal norms, Quinn launched into a dance—a madcap cavalcade of limbs and flailing poncho. His movements were a mosaic of folly and freedom. Absurd? Absolutely. Endearing? Irrevocably so.

Against my more restrained instincts, he lassoed me into his ecstatic whirlwind with an over-dramatized flick of his wrist. I mustered a look of theatrical disdain, an eye-roll garnished with a smirk, but there was no masking the rapture that was building within me.

You see, I had always been an oasis of calm surrounded by hurricanes—a stoic epicentre where emotions came to dissipate. But Quinn?...

He was the tempest incarnate, a swirling maelstrom of feels I had barricaded myself against for years. And as we sloshed through puddles, rain sluicing down our cheeks, it felt as if the universe itself had hit pause, allowing us a brief hiatus from reality.

For the first time in what felt like eons, I let go. I relinquished control. Gone were the barriers, the calculated guards. Instead, we were nothing but vibrations—melody, rain, and the tactile sensation of wet cobblestones underfoot blending into an ephemeral symphony. Our souls seemed to dance in tandem, as if choreographed by the whims of some cosmic maestro.

Lines demarcating the performer from the person I hid within began to dissolve. The falling rain became a solvent, melting away layers of artifice, leaving behind a kernel of unfiltered emotion.

Eyes closed, I surrendered to the crescendo. Each drop of rain was like a percussionist, every musical note a conductor, and each unspoken sentiment formed an ensemble. Time became abstract; we were not just ephemeral figures swallowed by an urban tempest. We were ageless, unfettered.

As the track's final notes evaporated into the damp air, the rain morphed into a listless drizzle. I couldn't help but glance towards an old mid-century furniture store across the street. The lights inside warmly contrasted the cool embrace of the rain, casting a gentle glow upon the well-crafted pieces from a bygone era. For a fleeting moment, our reflections in the store's window caught my eye, dancing in tandem with the stylish furnishings. Hinting at a different story.

I imagined us, not dancing in the rain, but lounging on that sleek couch, sipping wine, laughing over shared stories. An image of potential mornings together with coffee on the elegant table, late-night conversations ensconced in those plush chairs.

My heart clenched with an unspoken yearning, a subtle whisper of what could be—a future both tantalizingly close yet so distant. A reckoning dawned on me. Quinn wasn't just bringing chaos into my life. He was making me feel irrevocably alive again.

With the downpour becoming torrential, we decided to take shelter within the nearest sanctuary, which so happened to be… a cathedral.

The soft echoing hum of hymns were strangely juxtaposed against the hurried, panting steps of Quinn, as he climbed the final flight to the sanctified hall.

The cathedral's stained glass cast kaleidoscopic patterns across the cold stone floor, and I couldn't help but steal glances at Quinn, who appeared as though he'd misinterpreted 'church attire' with 'boonies construction worker.'

Decked out in muddy jeans and a white tank that caught every shaft of coloured light, he looked more like he was ready to lead the Village People than to attend a solemn mass.

But I couldn't say anything. Not when my own outfit was a mesh of leather and lace, skirting the blasphemous edge of divine decorum. In a room full of consecrated silences and veiled glances, we were a walking paradox. It was clear we were both out of our element, and that made the situation even more amusing.

We tiptoed, each to our chosen aisles, looking as out of place as a pair of peacocks in a parliament of owls. The atmosphere was thick with solemnity, a canvas begging to be defiled. It became an unspoken duel— facial expressions contorted into comic caricatures, poses struck with melodramatic flair, each of us laying a silent bet on who'd break into laughter first.

Latin incantations rolled off the altar, each syllable a time-honoured pebble in the sea of liturgical grandeur. But there we were, the incorrigible two—exchanging sidelong glances, batting back stifled giggles, and playing footsie under the benediction of centuries-old wooden pews.

A playful jab, a suggestive wink, an exaggerated roll of the eyes. Even as the congregation lined up in reverential quietude, we sensed our time was up. Not from a lack of respect for the sacred, but from the inevitable realization that we were an incendiary device set to blow in a tinderbox of piety.

So we made our exit. Outside, the weight of the atmosphere lifted, replaced by the chirping of birds and distant city sounds.

I smirked, breaking the brief silence between us. "'God, you're weird.'"

Quinn chuckled, casting a mischievous look. "Takes a weirdo to know a weirdo!"

Our irreverent pilgrimage to the cathedral was many things, a profane circus in a temple of hushed veneration, but most importantly, it was an affirmation. A confirmation that the spark between us wasn't just electric—it was divine, sacrilegious, and irrevocably binding. And as the reality settled in, a singular thought echoed through my mind.

Holy fuck was I screwed.

♡ CATS, CHATS & RATS. ♡

"Hunting season's nice this year"

Backstage Jacqueline's always smelled of burnt hair, fresh paint, and a hint of jasmine. It was a wild, heady cocktail that hit your senses like a freight train. Where dreams met desperation.

Makeup brushes, all in various stages of decay, littered the countertops, jostling for space with wigs of all colours and shades. Yet amidst all the clutter, the one thing that stood out was a starlet vanity, its mirror scribbled with **Vixen** in audacious red lipstick. Claiming it.

I'd just begun the surreptitious task of sliding a rather affluent client's wallet, along with a few other sparkly trinkets, into my secret stash when Angel's voice, dripping with that habitual condescension, hit my ears.

"Hey Vixen—"

Fuck, I nearly broke the drawer slamming it shut. Angel always had a knack for timing; like a feral cat, she knew just when to pounce.

She had this aura, Angel did. Like she always knew something you didn't. It was unnerving, and right now, she was exuding it in spades. She threw a bag at me, its contents clinking mysteriously.

"Aw, Hun," I began, a smirk creeping across my face, "I know I've been quite the cash cow for this place, but a bonus? This early in the game? You shouldn't have."

Angel's eyes held a playful malevolence. "Who's Jay?" she asked, deliberately casual.

That name detonated like dynamite in my ears. How did Angel know about Jay? My mind whirled in a cyclone of speculation and dread.

Jay was an enigma, sure, but he was also dangerous—both to himself and to anyone connected to him. He had skeletons in his closet that made my own look like cute accessories. If she knew about my debts… fuck!

And then the thought struck me like a thunderbolt—Emma Royd. Angel and Emma were as thick as thieves. If Angel knew, then Emma might as well have the news written in neon lights above her head. If she found out, she wouldn't just sing like a canary; she'd orchestrate a damn opera of exposure.

My nails dug into the palm of my hand, each crescent-shaped imprint a reminder of how quickly things could spiral out of control. I desperately needed to remain calm. Whatever the cost, I had to contain this before it ripped apart everything I'd carefully constructed.

My hand, already plundering the bag, froze mid-dive, bumping into what felt like Bambi's cat ear headphones. My mind vaulted into overdrive.

Fuck.

A litany of potential scenarios cascaded through my brain, each more disastrous than the last. In one, Angel and Emma teamed up to publicly expose not only me but also Jay, turning us in to the feds. In another, Jay's threat came back to haunt us, ensnaring Bambi in a web of dangers he couldn't even begin to comprehend. And in yet another, it was Bambi who became the unwitting fulcrum of all this chaos, his carefree life upended because he happened to be in the wrong place at the wrong time—namely, anywhere near me.

I felt the slick texture of the headphones under my fingers, but my mind barely registered the sensation. I was too wrapped up in an inner storm of overthinking, each flash of insight breeding more questions, more fears, and absolutely no answers.

I shot her a defiant look, but Angel was one step ahead.

"He dropped it off a minute ago," she drawled, smirking as she narrated the encounter, "What an interesting guy. He and I had a little... chat."

Instant panic. My mind flashed a slideshow of incriminating images—Jay's scars, his shitty tattoos... his intimate familiarity with me, all of it.

Fuck. Fuck. Fuck.

"Vixen," Angel's tone turned glacial, "Who's... Jay?"

I fumbled, trying to form a coherent response. My mind raced. The scent of jasmine grew overpowering. "A client," I muttered, praying she would buy the lie.

She glared me down, smirking. As I kept fumbling for words, I finally blurted, "I—need to... take some pics." Bolting upwards, I added, "He'll want to see me wearing this."

Before I could brace myself, the obnoxious 'ding' of a text notification rang out from my pocket. A cold dread settled in my chest. I didn't need to check to know who it was from. But I did anyway.

(The Devil): **Hunting season's nice this year**

In a tidal wave of panic, I grabbed the bag and bolted. Angel might have said something, yelled maybe, but the blood rushing in my ears drowned her out.

As I stumbled through the heavy red doors into the blinding light, all I could think of was one thing:

Where the fuck was Bambi?

My escape led me into the scorched expanse of Jacqueline's parking lot, the sun descending like an executioner's blade. The asphalt exuded a burnt rubber reek, mingling with the acrid bite of gasoline. It was the olfactory equivalent of a dumpster fire—utterly fitting for the psychic maelstrom clawing through my guts.

My phone, cradled desperately between ear and shoulder, was my sole anchor to sanity. Every ring felt like a dagger.

"Pick up. Pick up. Pick the fuck up," I silently incanted, as if I could hex the sound waves into dragging Bambi to the line.

My heart beat like a trapped bird in a cage. The weight of too many secrets threatened to crush me. I needed Bambi. His voice. The anchor he'd unknowingly become. Just one sign to prove he was okay, to make all this bearable.

As the deafening silence of the phone ring droned on, I felt the ground tilt. The glaring sun, the sounds of distant traffic, everything began to swirl into a disorienting blur.

And then, the world went silent.

The voicemail. "Hey Girl! You've reached Bambi. I'm out right now. Probs getting my hair done or something sexy. I'll call ya right back."

His voicemail was so distinctly Bambi—vivacious, irreverent, dripping with sass. Yet, today, it sounded ominous.

No. What have I done...

Fury and panic welled up in equal measure. I slammed my fist on the asphalt, cursing my choices, cursing Jay, cursing the universe.

But then, salvation. The soft, pulsating buzz of an—
INCOMING CALL FROM BAMBI

"H-Hey?" My voice quivered, desperate for the normalcy his voice promised.

"Hey! Sorry Babe! I was doing my nails and hair at the same time. Had to express dry them and ugh… chaos."

Drawing in a breath to steady myself, I asked, "You good?"

He responded with his typical flair. "I mean, other than having a horrible manicure right now, yeah…" A pause lingered, long enough for me to detect his underlying concern. "Why?"

I swallowed hard, the lump in my throat stubborn. "Just checking in," I lied. Or maybe it wasn't a complete lie? I really was just checking in, albeit spurred by paranoia and looming dread.

The words "just checking in" sounded like the biggest farce, an understatement as glaring as the midday sun. But what could I say? That I was fucking terrified?

Sighing, I added, "I'm coming over tonight, okay? I have some good news."

Just when, the pearl necklace around my neck suddenly felt cold and heavy. And, however loose it may have actually been, I somehow felt it ensnare me. Squeezing. Tighter.

♡ CONFESSIONS OF ♡ A LOLLIPOP-A-HOLIC.

"Have you ever been truly, madly loved?"

In the sequestered sanctum of backroom number six, with walls that had witnessed countless whispered confessions and clandestine rendezvous, Kitty and I stretched out on the bed, gazing at the languidly turning ceiling fan. Below the fan's hypnotic whirl, green and red neon lights flickered from the ceiling, bathing us in a synthetic aurora borealis, casting everything in sharp, high contrast, amid the gentle drone of 'Richmond Bridge' playing from an 80s turntable.

"How the HECK is this thing always right?" Kitty's voice, edged with a mix of frustration and wonder, sliced through the near trance, waving the tarot cards in her hand for emphasis.

A low chuckle unfurled from my lips as I swirled my cocktail. "The cards never lie."

She smirked, inching closer with her signature cherry lollipop in hand. Her talisman—or at least the talisman I had grown to associate her with.

Lollipop smack!

I could feel her magnetic energy drawing me in, as much as she was lured into my mysterious world. "Why do you always ask for everyone's birthday?"

Kitty's inquiry resonated in the labyrinth of my mind. Why did I always ask for everyone's birth date? It was more than a conversational quirk; it was a meticulously crafted stratagem, a key that had unlocked doors and hearts, alike.

This tactic was my guarded defence in a world where I had learned, sometimes brutally, that not everyone saw the poetry in chaos or the beauty in disaster. People wanted symmetry, patterns, predictability—something my inherently turbulent existence could seldom offer. So, the birth dates became my Rosetta Stone, translating the foreign terrains of human psychology into a language I could not only understand but also manipulate. But to speak it aloud, to grant someone that portal into my internal machinations?

Was it vulnerability or an unintended candidness triggered by an elusive sense of safety in Kitty's presence? Or maybe, it was the thrill of sharing a trade secret with another wandering spirit—much like the rebels of a bygone era sharing contraband codes under the cover of night. In that concealed cradle of neon light and spinning ceiling fans, I'd inadvertently let Kitty in—into a private chamber of my labyrinthine psyche that even I seldom visited.

I drew a shaky breath, my voice lowering, heavy with the pain of countless untold stories. "I guess I can let YOU in on the secret." The raw vulnerability in that confession was palpable. "It tells me how to act around you."

Kitty's gaze faltered. "What?"

Pushing past the knot in my throat, I let her into a corner of my mind. "Birth charts. They're like manuals. They tell me whether to make out with you or buy you a drink first, whether to feed you some kind of poetry or bullshit, if your love language is physical touch or not— all depending on your zodiac placements. It reveals your personality traits—like following a guideline, so people…" I paused, "Like me."

Silence stretched between us, filled with unspoken thoughts. "A little manipulative, isn't it?" she mused.

Wincing, I tried to defend, "Well, it's like adapting—or mirroring actually, what people want. Plus, you know," a shadow of a smirk, a defence mechanism. "It secures me a generous tip."

Our laughter felt liberating. Bright yet underscored with sadness. Echoing between us.

"Genius! You escorting witch. You gotta teach me!", Kitty exclaimed before her voice dropped an octave. "So… you're enjoying this?"

Feeling cornered, I attempted levity, "Hun, I'm not straight, but if you slip a little hundred in my garter, who knows what I could enjoy." I winked, "I might even fake an orgasm for you."

Her face softened, looking past the façade. "I meant this place, Dummy. This life. Are you happy?" A probing needle.

Happy…

As Kitty's voice hung in the air, that simple, four-letter word—happy—echoed within the confined walls of my mind like a riddle with no clear solution. What did it mean to be happy? The question hit, derailing my carefully assembled train of thought, tossing cargo of memories, emotions, and reflections into disarray.

For someone who had built a life on the alchemy of appearance and reality, the concept of happiness was as elusive as grabbing hold of smoke with bare hands. Was it the applause that roared like a lion every time I killed it on stage? Or the scent of a stranger, a fleeting intimacy that promised nothing more than ephemeral solace? Or perhaps it was hidden in those rare, quiet moments when I could drop the mask and breathe, however briefly, in the presence of a kindred spirit like… Quinn.

Each of these moments flashed across the panorama of my consciousness, challenging my understanding of a word so casually tossed around by the world. And in that split second, I came to a startling realization: I didn't know. I didn't know what happiness was anymore because I'd been too busy fantasizing about what it should look like.

Lollipop smack!

Kitty's question floated there, begging for a candid response. Yet, as I looked into her eyes, I felt a peculiar solidarity. Here we were, two souls intersecting in a world of endless facades, pondering the same existential quandary in the silence that spoke volumes.

I sighed, looking at the neon lights above. "It'll do…" I paused for a brief second, before adding, "other than Angel having bitch mode activated by default."

Kitty seemed lost in thought. Suddenly, she pulled out two cards—**The Empress** and **The Wheel of Fortune**. "Angel can be… reactive… but she's just protecting us, y'know."

Her voice softened as she looked at the cards. "What does it mean?"

I leaned in and pointed to **The Empress**. "Angel—Authoritative demon witch. Likes to be in control of everything… but protects those around her. An Empress." I then pointed to **The Wheel of Fortune**. "This one's karma. She definitely brings karmic justice to everyone around her… including you."

Kitty's face fell, memories threatening to spill from her eyes. She swallowed hard, trying to steady herself.

Knowing damn well the tale, I pushed, "What happened?"

The weight of my words pressed down on Kitty. Memories seemed to dance in her eyes, "You know how it goes… girl meets boy, falls for his charm. He tells her about his 'great' idea of a business... and she's the star of the show—for a while..." her joyful expression dwindles down, "but then... he becomes violent. She runs away, and does the only thing she's ever known."

My eyes softened, holding a pain that mirrored hers. "Yeah... heard that story before."

Lollipop smack!

Pushing through the heavy atmosphere, Kitty continued, fiddling with her lollipop, "Well, Angel saved me from that—life on the streets. She taught me, showed me her ways, changed everything."

I gave her a small, knowing smile. Trying to shift the mood, Kitty cheekily flung her lollipop out of her mouth, raised her leg, and showed off her ten-inch platform stiletto. "And saved me from the delusion that I could work the streets all alone in THESE."

A moment passed between us, filled with unspoken words, soft laughter and shared experiences. But then, Kitty dropped her bomb, "Have you ever been truly loved like that, Vixen?"

Loved—

Before I could muster the strength to answer, my timer, always mercilessly punctual, shattered the moment.

Clearing the emotion from my voice, I rallied, "Well, if you don't mind, Hun, I've got some closeted kitty cats to tend to."

I winked, giving her a peck on the cheek before slipping back into the night's rhythm.

With a last lingering glance, charged with a myriad of emotions, I stepped back into the shadows of Jacqueline's.

Loved? Of course I've been loved... yeah.

♡ GAY 4 PAY. ♡

"Is this fucking appetizing enough for you?"

The bathroom at Jacqueline's always had this peculiar blue glow. It was supposed to be soothing, but it just made me feel like I was trapped in an underwater cave. The lights refracted off the damp, white tiles and the large, aged mirror on the wall. It was hard to believe that this was where I fixed up, where I prepped for the next part of the night.

As I touched up my makeup, I pocketed a wristwatch I had "inherited" from my latest, particularly tipsy, client. Another trophy for my collection—a silent, shimmering secret. But—

As I stared into my reflection, my mind unexpectedly somersaulted back to Kitty's probing words—had I ever been loved like that? The question had been lingering in the recesses of my mind, scratching at something tender and raw, and now it burst forth, unbidden.

An irrational, searing anger rose from a place deep within me, clouding my thoughts like a wildfire. It was as though Kitty's innocent question had unwittingly detonated an emotional landmine, sending fragments of something I couldn't quite identify into the air. Was it resentment? Grief? Buried trauma? I couldn't pinpoint it, but it felt like a serrated blade scraping against my heart.

What right did she have to ask me something so intimate? Did she think she had unraveled my labyrinthine complexity, just by reading a couple of tarot cards and sharing a vulnerable moment?

I sneered internally, anger simmering. Sure, I asked for people's birth dates, read their signs, projected the person they wanted me to be. But all of that was a facade, wasn't it? A way to protect myself from questions exactly like this one.

Fury contorted within me like a cyclone, indistinct and faceless. It seemed to radiate outwards, changing the energy in the room. Just when—

The bathroom door burst open with such violence it was as if a gust of wind had torn through the room, unsettling the damp, stagnant air. It was Aspen, and his entrance was a spectacle in itself—a living embodiment of menace.

He was taller than most, shaved army man head and his physique—a contradictory mix of lean muscle and litheness, like a predator perfectly tuned for both power and speed. His angular face was twisted into a scowl, eyes aflame with incandescent rage that seemed to light up the cave-like blue hue of the bathroom.

Silver rings clinking!

But what really caught the eye were his hands—those furious, clenched fists. Adorned with silver rings that shimmered in the weird lighting, each piece of jewelry seemed like an extension of his wrath, a material echo of his inner turmoil. It was as if each ring was a marker, a commemorative coin, for every grudge he held, every battle he'd fought, whether won or lost. His talismans.

"Are you for REAL, Dude?" Anger was evident in every syllable.

Those hands of his, they closed the distance between us in an instant, gripping my collar with a palpable intensity, as his rings bit into the fabric like tiny teeth. And as they did, the contrast between his furious force and my own spiralling emotions was stark—a collision of two hellscapes in a room too small to contain them.

Before I knew it, he yanked my makeup brush from my hand and pinned me against the porcelain sink. "Whoa, take it easy," I countered.

Silver rings clinking!

"As if I care about your fucking contour!" Aspen snarled, his grip tightening on my collar. His rings digging into my skin. "You've been hijacking my clients. ZERO bookings for me this week, and guess what? Somehow, they've ALL switched to YOU!"

I looked him straight in the eye, my gaze icy but electrifying. "Well, Hun, not to burst your ego, but maybe it's because I offer a certain je ne sais quoi that you clearly lack."

Then, just to throw some glitter on this dumpster fire, I popped a pink pill from the stash in my pocket. "Maybe they just find me more... appetizing," I said, the word dripping from my tongue like venom as I crunched down on the pill.

Foot tapping. My knuckles cracking. *Silver ring clinking!*

For a terrifying moment, I felt the eye-twitch, the barely-contained rage in Aspen's gaze. For a split second, I had the bizarre sensation of being teleported inside his enraged mind—unhinged fantasies swirled around me like a tornado, each more violent than the last. Witnessing his violent daydream.

The light in the bathroom twisted and spiralled like a circus show, throwing shadows that danced in my vision like I was peering through a deranged looking glass of wonders. It wasn't just disorienting; it was a damn spectacle, a high-wire act with no safety net.

Aspen's breaths transformed, becoming guttural growls that seemed to blend seamlessly with the surreal acoustics of the room. Then, in a swift whirlwind of movement that felt choreographed in its violence, he snatched a fistful of my mullet and yanked me toward the toilet. Panic surged through me, but everything felt distant and detached, as if I was watching a horror movie rather than being in it.

His grip tightened, forcing my head into the cold embrace of the toilet bowl. The world dimmed to a disorienting medley of muffled sounds and underwater visions. I could feel the cold ceramic and the pressure of his boot on the back of my neck. I tried to resist, but his strength was overpowering. I could see his calf muscles tense and bulging.

"LIKE THE TASTE, HUH? IS THIS FUCKING APPETIZING ENOUGH FOR YOU?," he roared, rage dripping from every syllable.

And then, he crossed another line in a night full of line-crossing. With a vile smirk, he unzipped his pants and committed the final act of degradation. A yellow stream splashed into the toilet, an affront to every shred of dignity left. But amid the roar and the rush, his voice cut through, teetering between mania and a sort of exultation. "AAAAAAAAH!"

It was the unhinged scream of a man teetering on the edge. Of what, I didn't know.

But as his voice echoed, bouncing off the dingy tiles and filling the cramped space, it mingled with my own emotions. Anger, humiliation, fear—they all swirled together in a volatile cocktail. And in that moment, the boundaries between Aspen and me, between predator and prey, seemed perilously thin.

Silver ring clinking!

But just as abruptly, I was thrust back to reality, the deafening sound in the room being the clinking of his rings against the sink. Tapping out an impatient beat. I felt the room's tension ratchet up to unbearable levels. The surreal quality of the bathroom lights made the brief daydream even more haunting. It was as though the room had become a chamber for our mirrored torments —a sanctuary for our collective demons, temporarily unleashed.

The silence that followed was deafening, and in that infinite second, I felt a chasm open within me, a void so deep that even Aspen's impending wrath seemed trivial in comparison.

I had to find a way to bury this inexplicable anger, this internal tempest, before it consumed me. I couldn't afford to lose myself to an emotion I couldn't even name.

As I steered my thoughts back to the immediate crisis, I clenched my jaw and readied myself for whatever Aspen would throw my way next. But Kitty's burning question, the one that had ignited something so fiercely uncontrollable within me, remained, smouldering in the depths of my soul. Had I ever been loved like that? And why did the question unsettle me so profoundly?

I could barely find my voice amidst my inner rage. But I needed to release, so I clapped back, "That toxic masculinity of yours? It's your own worst enemy, you know," I clawed my way to find my voice, "it scares everyone away, Hun."

He stared me down for what felt like an eternity before releasing my now-crushed mesh top. I couldn't help but voice my annoyance. "Jesus! They don't make these anymore, Neanderthal." I said, trying to reclaim the space, pointing at the small tear in it.

As Aspen stomped away without a word, a familiar sound echoed—

Ping!

PrideMate. At it again, with its impeccable timing. "Yeah, yeah. I'm coming," I muttered to my reflection, fluffing up my mullet with a flick of the wrist.

I took a moment to gather the shards of my splintered composure, casting one last glance at the blue-lit mirror, as if expecting it to answer that unsettling question.

♡ FALLEN ANGEL. ♡

"He'll be the end of you. I promise you that"

Smoke spiralled like an exotic dancer in the air as I swayed into Emma Royd's boudoir, the weight of fresh, crisp bills in my pocket transforming every step into a strut worthy of Paris Fashion Week. "I'm taking off tonight—"

Bubble gum pop!

Angel's voice ripped through the air like a flare gun, derailing my exit speech. "He's got a FUCKING PIMP! He's fucking us OVER, Mama!" Her words were sharp knives, slashing through the room's moody ambience.

A pulse of cold dread stabbed through my veins. Outed. Right here, in the sanctity of Emma's boudoir.

The pause was fractional, nearly imperceptible, a nanosecond where the future—my future—teetered on the edge. But panic is a messy bitch, and she wasn't about to ruin my makeup.

Arching an eyebrow, I tried to play it cool, deflecting. "Well, I probably won't send him a Christmas card anymore either, but…" A smirk tugged at the corner of my lips, "That's no way to talk about Aspen."

Bubble gum pop!

Angel's eyes, twin furnaces, locked onto mine. "TELL. HER," she seethed, her voice a striking hiss of molten anger.

As if I had all the time in the world, my fingers leisurely ventured into my pocket, resurfacing with a pack of StarChews.

She continued on. "Tell her about Jay—"

Fuck. Now I really had to sell it. I had no other choice… I had to pretend Jay was more angel than demon, even though every fibre in my being screamed in revolt at the thought. Acting was a part of the game, sure, but this? This would be my magnum opus, a performance that would either save me or doom me.

"My client?" I quipped, pulling out an unfortunate yellow piece and curling my lip. "Ew. Here," I extended the vile candy towards Angel, every move dripping with feigned sweetness. "I hate these ones."

She remained stone-faced, so I shrugged, retracting the offer.

"He and I go way back," I drawled, easing onto the crushed velvet couch's armrest, a picture of casual defiance. "He treated me to the finest dinners, and oh, those secluded beachfront villas. Draped me in luxury like a cat in silk," I chuckled, letting my gaze wander, as if bored.

More like Denny's as his idea of high-end cuisine.

Jay's name a red hot brand searing through mind. I hated him; hated that he held any power over me, and I loathed myself for having to defend him. But the alternative—exposure, shame, the unraveling of my carefully spun web—wasn't an option. I had to play the hand I was dealt, even if it made my skin crawl.

Catching her piercing stare again, I continued, forcing each word out like it was a mouthful of broken glass. "I mean, sure, he's a bit... raw. But he'd never hurt a fly."

He'd slowly burn them with a magnifying glass, actually.

As I popped a cherry StarChew, savouring the victory of the flavour, Angel's exasperation exploded. "You. Fucking. LIAR." She swiped the pack, sending candy missiles across the room.

Gritting my teeth beneath my feigned smirk, I shot back, "We've all had our share of 'complex' clients, Hun."

She hissed, "I know a fucking PIMP when I see one! We've all had one like him!"

Deftly, I popped a pink pill from its clandestine hiding place and let it dissolve on my tongue.

Our words hung in the air, a precarious constellation of truths and lies. Angel glared, eyes ablaze, but the fires had shifted—no longer an inferno, but the smouldering embers of a battle hard fought and lost.

It was a pyrrhic victory, one that left me questioning the cost. I felt dirty, tainted by the forced veneration of a man who embodied all the shadows I sought to escape. But as the silence stretched, pregnant with unspoken confessions and bitter realizations, I donned my mask of aloofness like a second skin.

Fists squeezing. My knuckles cracking. *Bubble gum pop!*

I could almost hear the thoughts racing in her mind, a feverish rush of emotions taking form. A daydream.

The atmosphere felt suddenly different, thickened with tension. Neon green light washed over the room, transforming Angel's face into a sinister tableau, each line etched with demonic intensity.

Crash!

With a sudden, savage movement, she shattered the nearest lamp. Glass shards flew in every direction like some abstract meteor shower, but one piece—oh, that one piece—captured her attention. She picked it up, her fingers wrapping around it in a grip that could only mean trouble.

Time froze as she turned her rage-filled gaze to me, lunging forward, a dark silhouette against the neon. The shard made contact with my neck, once, twice—the cold sting of it contrasting with the warmth of the blood that started to flow.

I watched in horror as I fell, the world tilting, the sounds muffling. Angel, triumphant and savage, stood over me, her face splattered with my blood, a grotesque mask of fury. Then, in a move so incongruous with the violence that had just unfolded, she brought a bloodied finger to her mouth and licked the shit out of it.

The taste seemingly cementing her victory.

Bubble gum pop!

With a swift motion, the room's energy shifted. Emma's voice tore through the tension, its timbre a guillotine's blade, "ENOUGH, ANGEL!" Bringing us all back to the tangible world.

I felt it, but I also felt strangely distant, as if I were watching a drama unfold on a stage far removed from me. And then, amid that psychic tension, something solid and real made contact with my face—a sharp, stinging slap. Angel's slap.

I barely registered it, confusing the sensation with the surreal violence of the daydream. The pain seemed to linger in the nebulous space between imagination and reality, unsettling in its ambiguity. But even as I questioned its existence, a part of me felt it was deserved, as if some cosmic justice had been meted out in that fleeting moment of contact.

Emma's tired gaze rested on Angel. With a heavy sigh, she stretched out a hand full of twenties. "Here's your pay for the week." The bills looked as forlorn and crumpled as the energy in the room, as if they too had been through the wringer.

"Wait, but it's only Tuesday…" Angel's voice held a tremor of bewilderment, her eyes flitting between the money and Emma's set face.

The room felt colder, the atmosphere denser. I tried to fade into the background, but the weight of Angel's gaze was inescapable.

"You're out Angel." Emma's voice was firm, leaving no room for debate.

"You're kidding me?" A laugh of disbelief escaped Angel's lips. "Me? You're cutting ME out?!" The incredulity in her voice was palpable.

She approached Emma, her every step echoing the storm brewing inside her. Their proximity was almost suffocating. "He'll be the end of you. I promise you that." Angel's voice dripped with venom.

Could she be right? A twinge of guilt stirred within me, only to be suppressed under layers of outward composure. But before I could articulate any semblance of a response, Angel spat her gum, landing it with spiteful precision on my boot. "You better watch yourself," she hissed before storming out.

As the door slammed behind her, the room seemed to take a collective breath, as if recovering from a near-death experience.

"Don't let her get to you. She's always been the jealous type," Emma said.

As she tried to console me, something clicked, a disquieting insight that made my stomach churn. I recalled the wad of cash she had handed Angel. Crumpled twenties. Meanwhile, my pocket was fat with fresh, crisp hundreds from tonight alone. I suddenly understood why Emma had taken my side so unequivocally. It wasn't loyalty, it wasn't personal attachment—no, it was something far more primitive. Money.

As these thoughts spiralled through my mind, Emma's voice became a distant murmur, her words meaningless syllables that did nothing to fill the growing void inside me. I smiled at her, the same practiced, hollow smile I'd given to countless clients, and excused myself.

I was the golden goose of Jacqueline's, and Emma Royd wouldn't risk losing that, not even for the sake of collective security. The very safety that Angel, in her rough, acerbic manner, was trying to protect. I looked at the door Angel had exited through, and in that moment, it hit me like a freight train—Kitty was right.

Angel had been the real mother of the house. Her ferociousness, her razor-sharp tongue, it wasn't petty jealousy or casual cruelty; it was a warped expression of love, an instinctual drive to protect the flock—Kitty, Aspen and herself—even when the shepherd was blinded by greed.

And what had I done? I had turned that flock against her, masked Jay's malevolence with honeyed lies, and cost her the sanctuary she had tried so hard to secure for us. For what? So I could keep my seat at a feast where everyone was ultimately on the menu?

But as I sat there, surrounded by the damning evidence of my own moral compromises, I shook my head. I couldn't afford to dwell on this, not if I wanted to keep my own flock—however small it may be—safe. My eyes fell on a shiny object on Emma's dresser—a mirror, reflecting an immaculate visage of fabricated self-assuredness.

I stared at myself, locked eyes, as if expecting the glass to whisper secrets back to me.

"I can't be the only villain here, right?" I muttered to my reflection. After all, Emma made her choices, Angel made hers, and every other girl in this place had her own bag of dirty little secrets. Why should I bear the brunt of collective blame?

The shadow of doubt and guilt danced at the edges of my mind. But like always, I quickly bottled it up, sealing it tight, determined not to let it break through.

♡ THE TWINK'S ♡ REPRIEVE.

"How's deer season going?"

The dull hum of city noise was all I could hear as I approached Bambi's apartment, replaying my little feud with Angel on loop—was I starting to collect lies like they were vintage Prada bags? That misfit had been genuine, perhaps the only 'real' soul in a world of pretence and fake eyelashes. And what had my tangled web of half-truths and lipgloss smirks cost her?

I shook my head, as if I could dislodge the thought.

Come on, Vixen, you're the main character here.

Casting the growing pile of mental laundry into a corner of my mind labeled "Deal With Later or Never," I snapped back into my radiant self just as something told me to pause before entering Bambi's unit.

So I did, pressing my ear to the cold door. It was a trick I'd picked up during my countless escapades, a trick that had saved me more than once from interrupting… things I did not wish to witness.

An orgasm of button mashing erupted from the other side. Classic Bambi. He was probably in the middle of one of his gaming sessions. I could almost picture him on that worn-out cloud-shaped couch, bathed in the glow of his rainbow LED gaming station, completely lost to the virtual world.

"EYY! GOTCHA, BITCH!" Bambi's voice came through, filled with that giddy triumph sprinkled with vulgarity he always had when he pulled off a win. It made me smirk. "The femboy does it again, fuckers! The supreme!"

I snickered, already envisioning him draped in virtual medals of honour. But then the insidious chime of an incoming comment unraveled my amusement.

"Show your bootie?" Bambi read aloud, groaning loudly, and even without seeing his face, I could almost see his eyes rolling so hard they'd unlock secret compartments in his brain. "Ew. Again with that? I'm not showing my ass, Sugartits twenty one…"

Another chime came through.

There was a tantalizing pause. My interest piqued.

"You'll tip me?" Bambi's voice rose, sweetening with the allure of cash. "How much are we talking here…"

Same ol' money whore.

I took a deep breath, refusing to let Bambi dig himself any deeper, and pushed the door open.

The scene was exactly as I'd pictured. Bambi, surrounded by pizza boxes, deep in his game, looked up as the door creaked, legs spread open. The monarch of his junk food realm. "Oh! Gotta go, Bee-bees!" He blew theatrical smooches into the webcam. "Mwah, Mwah, Mwah! 'Til the next virtual sin-fest!"

The stream died as he wheeled around, flashing me that patented grin of mischief.

"Had fun?" I smirkingly delivered. A broken controller in the bin caught my eye. "Looks like you had a bit of a rage session?" I quipped, deflecting his attention from the exhaustion I was sure my face betrayed.

Bambi chortled, clutching a slice of pizza as if it were his royal sceptre. "One day without the cat ears... ONE DAY... and everyone loses their minds."

I fiddled with my nails, searching for a way to change the subject, but Bambi was too sharp. "You checked your place, right? They aren't there?"

A lump clawed at my throat, as I remembered Jay's threat. The cat ears carefully placed at the bottom of that bag... I looked away briefly, a weight settling in my chest. And shook my head. I couldn't add anymore stress to Bambi's already heightened anxiety.

"Hey..." I began, reaching into my bag and pulling out the disco ball, hoping the sight of the hidden cash inside would divert our conversation from the dangers I'd been dodging all night. Bambi's curious gaze locked onto it, and I simply said, "Open it."

Bambi reached into the disco ball, and as he pulled out the huge pile of cash, his eyes widened, almost bulging from their sockets. "No. Freaking. Way?!" he exclaimed, his voice filled with disbelief.

I nodded, a knowing smirk on my lips. The night's ordeal seemed to have paid off. Ah, the scent of freshly laundered money mixed with a dash of peril—the only cologne that mattered.

Bambi let out an exaggerated sigh of relief, falling back onto the plush, cloud-like couch. "OH! THANK OUR LESBIAN GODDESS!" He covered his face with his hands momentarily before pulling them away, his eyes sparkling with tears of relief. "It's over—it's… finally. Over."

The ambience of the room changed, the tension melting away. Wanting to distract us further from the night's events, I reached into my bag and pulled out my tarot cards. I began shuffling them, enjoying the soft, rhythmic sound. "It sure is."

My eyes glanced at the wads of cash now safely stashed away, and I felt this unspoken wave of relief flood over me. I'd done it. I'd scrounged together enough to pay back Jay and end that sordid chapter of my life. As the weight of constant anxiety lifted off me, it felt like I was floating, soaring above a world that was coloured in not just fifty, but a million shades of grey.

However, just as I was about to fully embrace the emotional equivalent of a bubble bath and champagne, my tarot cards had another message. As I shuffled, one slid out of the deck as if propelled by an unseen force.

The Hanged Man.

A man suspended upside-down, his face oddly serene but his hands bound behind his back. It was a card that often symbolized feeling trapped, letting go, or a change of perspective. Confusion stirred within me, like a drop of ink muddying clear water. I frowned at the ominous sign when an unexpected sound broke my concentration.

Ping!

I glanced at the PrideMate notification.

(Quinn): **Hello, Dolly. How's deer season going?**

I couldn't help but smile, casting a quick glance at Bambi. He was sporting a baby blue hoodie, one that had probably seen the inside of a washing machine as often as a vampire sees daylight. His short shorts were an eye-watering shade of pink, leaving little to the imagination and doing nothing to hide his unfortunately "meaty tuck." Bambi's whole ensemble screamed 'I woke up like this, and I have zero intentions of changing,' with a side note of 'Yes, fashion police, you might want to start drafting that warrant.' Typing back the obvious, I smirked.

(Me): **As meaty as ever**

Bambi's voice cut through my brief distraction. "For a sec there, I REALLY thought I was a goner…"

Ping!

(Quinn): **Come over!**

(Me): **I'm busy, Hun.**

Bambi's dramatics knew no end. "I was actually considering escaping to Alaska!"

Ping!

(Quinn): **Please?**

With the begging face emoji.

Bambi continued, "I was THAT desperate, Vixen—ALASKA!"

I chuckled, trying to stifle my laughter.

(Me): **That emoji won't get you very far with me...**

Ping!

(Quinn): **How about now?**

There it was, right next to his begging plea—a cowboy emoji.

I felt the colour rise to my cheeks. It was stupid, really. I mean, it was just an emoji, a simple digital caricature, right? But it wasn't just any emoji; it was THE cowboy emoji. That tiny cartoon cowboy had become a sort of inside joke between us. Quinn had used it so often it had started to feel like a symbol of him—rugged, a bit old-fashioned, and charming in a way that was hard to ignore.

This lil' shit.

It was oddly romantic, a tiny pixelated cowboy roping in my emotional defences, something no string of poetic words had ever managed to do.

I smirked, now feeling a little giddy, a little exposed but also... happy, as Bambi suddenly became more animated. "So now what?..." But I was fixed to my screen.

(Me): **Tempting...**

When Bambi interrupted with a, "who are you texting?"

Completely disconnected from him, my reflexes kicked in. "That's crazy—" as my voice trailed off.

"Vixen... who are you texting?" Bambi's eyes twinkled with mischief.

As I looked up, dazed from the messages, a smile curving my lips, I found Bambi staring intently at me, his smug grin threatening to split his face.

Fuck.

Tap. Tap. Tap. He tapped his finger rhythmically on the couch, not breaking eye contact.

"You lying little bitch," Bambi accused playfully.

No. No. NO—

"The day has finally come…" he went on.

Don't say it!

"You're seeing someone," he concluded with the biggest grin I had ever seen.

Suddenly, he sprang up with the energy of a released spring, running around the room frantically, his dramatic flair fully unleashed.

With every leap and turn, he looked like a rogue Easter egg brought to life, throwing a tantrum because no one had found him during the Easter Hunt. But that was Bambi—larger than life, brighter than a box of Crayolas, and a forever-clashing cacophony of colours and moods that made you wonder what a unicorn on speed might feel like.

"NO—no, no, no! I'm-It's—not that." My efforts to calm him were in vain as Bambi's voice continued to fill the room, "It's the apocalypse! Quick! Take cover!" He cried out, grabbing his wigs and holding them close, "SAVE THE WIGS!"

Suppressing my laughter was proving to be a difficult task. I watched as Bambi theatrically zipped around, his antics trying to cover up my own surprise and flustered state.

The truth was, Quinn's text did make my heart race a little faster, and having Bambi find out about it only intensified the excitement, mingling it with a touch of embarrassment. But, like any good performer, I wasn't about to let my mask slip.

"Relax, will you?" I chuckled, attempting to downplay it all. Inside, however, I felt giddy, like a teen with their first crush. It was a sensation I hadn't allowed myself to feel in a while.

Bambi seemed to read a bit of this, his eyes still gleaming with mischief, but I bottled up the feeling, pushing it deep down. "You're overthinking it," I waved him off.

Just then, my phone buzzed again:

INCOMING VIDEO CALL FROM QUINN

Are you fucking kidding me.

Bambi's eyebrows shot up. "A VIDEO CALL!—Ew! Who does that?! This is serious!"

I couldn't stop blushing, "NO. He's just a client." I quickly stowed away my phone. "He's… a little weird." I yanked Bambi off the couch, "Open the computer. We're streaming. NOW."

Bambi groaned, "Oh god no! I'M streaming. You'd only ruin my streak… and probably show your ass—Get yourself an OnlyFans, girl."

Shaking my head, I laughed, "Bitch." I nudged him playfully, twirling the disco ball in my hand.

And in that moment, amid our dramatics and escapades, his outfit's psychedelic vibes were the perfect antidote to my lingering thoughts about Angel, Jay… The Hanged Man. Bambi was my lifeline, always pulling me back to the surface whenever I started to drift too deep into the abyss of my own mind.

As I glanced once more at my phone, the edges of my mouth involuntarily crept up into a smile.

I would never say it out loud…

But there was a spark of happiness inside. Maybe, just maybe, it was okay to feel this way. But for now, I had a an over-dramatic twink to entertain.

♡ FIGHT OR FLIGHT ♡ STARRY NIGHTS.

"You'll be the death of me, Quinn"

The corridor outside of Bambi's apartment was bathed in a quiet serenity. The wafting scent of decaying wallpaper and something distinctly earthy greeted my senses, a stark contrast to Bambi's saccharine bubblegum paradise.

As I stepped out of the colourful anime dream pad, Bambi's voice, tinged with genuine concern, echoed from the doorframe. "Please call me before you give Jay the money," he urged, his fingers still lingering on the door, "I don't want you to be alone with him."

"I will," I assured him, already feeling the weight of the situation pressing down on me.

Bambi hesitated, his typically cheeky eyes now soft with worry. "Okay… later, Babe. Love ya."

The door clicked shut behind me, casting a shadow that mixed with the cool blue hues of the hallway lights. I started towards the stairs, every step echoing in the silent space, but a sudden impulse had me halt in my tracks. The door next to Bambi's place beckoned.

With a heart pounding against the cage of my chest, I made a quick U-turn and slipped into the unit next door: Quinn's.

The atmosphere of Quinn's apartment bedroom was ethereal, almost as if I had stepped inside a living, breathing Van Gogh canvas. Above, the full moon illuminated the room in a wash of cool blue, painting silvery traces on every surface. Stars twinkled through the window, each one competing for attention, yet collectively creating a spectacle of beauty.

The room felt like a peek into Quinn's soul—deep mahoganies, rich burgundies, and tantalizing blacks. Everything from the worn-out leather couch that sat by the window to the mysterious artifacts placed strategically on wooden shelves, everything screamed Quinn.

And there, on the bedside table, lay his cowboy hat—its appearance uncannily resembling the very emoji he often sent. The universe's sense of humour, it seemed, was in fine form tonight. A chuckle escaped my lips.

Picking up the hat, I momentarily donned it, tilting it rakishly over one eye, imagining myself as the outlaw of this modern Wild West. The texture, the smell, it was intoxicating.

My skin was slick with a gentle sheen of perspiration, the aftermath of our shared closeness. I found solace in the rhythmic thump of Quinn's heart, lying on his bare chest. My fingers unconsciously traced infinity loops over the expanse of his skin, finding their way through the familiar maze of scars, muscle, and warmth—a dance on the contours of his being.

The gentle slope of his collarbone, leading to the defined expanse of his chest, held stories of perseverance. My fingers traced the chiseled planes, feeling the tautness of his pecs. Each muscle was a chapter, and I revelled in the sensation, exploring further.

Moving lower, I encountered the ripple of his abs, each one standing proud, yet seamlessly blending into the next, like a series of cascading waterfalls.

The faint trail of hair that led from his navel downwards was a path less traveled, inviting and mysterious. As my fingers ventured, they brushed against the rough patches of scars, each a badge of honour from life's battles, contrasting beautifully against the smoothness of his skin.

Every dip and ridge felt like braille, narrating tales of determination, joy, pain, and resilience. Quinn's body was a symphony of perfection and flaws, creating a harmonious blend that was profoundly human. As I continued my dance, I marvelled at the balance of power and vulnerability beneath my touch. Every infinity loop was a celebration, an acknowledgment of the man he was and the journey he had undertaken.

Quinn's voice, deep and imbued with curiosity, resonated in the hushed room. "What do you want?"

Grinning, I teased, "Trying to decode me, cowboy?"

His ensuing laughter was hearty, infectious, and echoed the very joy of living. "In life," he clarified. "Your biggest desire. The ultimate dream."

I found myself lost in contemplation.

What do I truly want?

A weighty silence enveloped me. My mind wandered. What did I truly want? The question seemed simple, but the answer...

I remembered those late nights, when the world around me slept, and I'd find solace in the glow of the television screen. The monochrome magic of old Hollywood movies played out before me—the glitz, the glam, the promise of a world far removed from mine. There was something inexplicably comforting in seeing those faces, full of hope and laughter, frozen forever in a time when things seemed simpler. Happier.

And then, there was Dolly. The vivacious protagonist from "Hello, Dolly!"—so full of life, energy, and passion. Not just loved because she was beautiful or witty, but for her spirit, her infectious zest for life. The way she'd light up a room just by being in it, the way people would gravitate towards her. That kind of happiness, that pure, unadulterated joy that wasn't tied to transactional affections—it was magnetic.

She was happy. And everyone—truly—loved her.

A love that wasn't masked by materialistic desires or hidden agendas. A love that wasn't paid for, but was freely given and received. It seemed like a distant dream, a fantastical notion from another era, but deep down, that yearning remained.

"To be like Dolly," I whispered, allowing myself that vulnerability, letting Quinn glimpse the depth of that desire. To be not just seen, but truly recognized. Not just admired, but genuinely loved. Not as a product, a facade, or a momentary distraction, but as a human being yearning for happiness and love in its purest form.

His eyes, those beautiful eyes, deep pools of emotion, searched mine. "Are you?"

I allowed a smirk, feeling the weight of everything I'd been through and everything I aimed for. "I'm definitely getting there."

Without a pause, he ventured into deeper territory. "And why escorting?"

I raised an eyebrow, feigning a look of mock outrage, "So many questions tonight."

Yet, his eyes, earnest and unwavering, those cerulean blues, begged an answer. "Everyone's career has something special to it," he murmured. "What makes yours all... worth it."

I took a moment, the gravity of the question sinking in. Each person I'd met, each story I'd been privy to, each moment of vulnerability and strength flashed through my mind. The reasons were many, and they were complex, but in that moment, under the watchful gaze of the moon, they felt simpler than ever.

I looked into his eyes, finding only curiosity and genuine interest. Taking a deep breath, I ventured, "You know how sometimes, when people confide in you… literally about anything—struggles, trauma—they cry, laugh, heal. And for a brief moment, you feel like you're rebuilding their entire confidence?" I began, my voice softening. "Well, that's escorting."

He looked at me, a hint of surprise flashing across his face. "Would ya look at that," he whispered, his voice filled with wonder, "deep DEEP down... you just want to be loved."

My breath caught in my throat. I hesitated, momentarily flustered. Using humour as a shield, I quipped, "no, I just like being a life coach, model, business owner, and actor."

Recovering, I leaned over, placing a gentle kiss on his cheek. "See," I whispered playfully, "I'm actually quite versatile." I chuckled softly, the edges of my lips curving up in amusement. "And I hear the pay ain't half bad. You should try."

Quinn pulled me closer, his warm breath fanning over my face. "I have all the man I need. So…" he squeezed me in a tight embrace, "I'm good for now."

I found myself getting lost in his eyes, feeling a pull I hadn't felt in a long time. The emotions swirling inside me were tumultuous, confusing, and exhilarating all at once.

"Why... me?" The question slipped out before I could stop it. A heavy beat of silence followed.

Fuck my life.

Desperately trying to reel it back in, "Okay—no. Never mind. I was just curious! That's fucking cheesy—you're just... from such a different world—" I took a second to regain my composure, "you've got everything figured out and you're so..." I looked up, deep into his ocean eyes, and, "why me?"

Quinn looked at me, his eyes searching mine. I wanted to look away, but I was trapped in his gaze.

He paused, his smirk deepening. "Are you kidding me?"

I stared at him, caught off-guard by the intensity in his gaze. "You are probably the most confident person I know. You rock your own world—to your own pace—unafraid of people's opinions or judgments... sure, you might be a little brash sometimes, but—," he let out a soft chuckle, "you shine, Vixen. You're lucky."

I felt my heart constrict, emotions threatening to overwhelm me. "I wish I was like you," he murmured, his fingers caressing my face.

The room seemed to contract, time warping around us. Every touch, every gaze was amplified, stirring an avalanche of emotions within me. I felt like I was caught in a maelstrom, a cyclone of conflicting sensations—intense longing, a fear of vulnerability, the sting of past betrayals, and the warmth of the moment.

Memories, both cherished and painful, flashed through my mind. Past lovers who'd left scars, moments of euphoria turned bitter by reality, laughter shared under starlit skies, and tears shed in the shadowy corners of solitude. The highs and lows of my life seemed to coalesce in that very room, battling for dominance.

As Quinn's fingers continued to trace the canvas of my skin, every touch sent electric jolts through me. Each one seemed to echo with a promise, a hope, a peril. There was a magic in the room, a raw, unbridled power that seemed to surge and pulse, drawing us even closer.

The overwhelming rush of feelings, the potent mix of our intertwined pasts and presents, the sheer intensity of the moment—it was suffocating, exhilarating, terrifying, and comforting all at once.

And for the first time in a long time, amidst the chaotic tapestry that was my life, I felt seen.

A lump formed in my throat, my voice trembling under the weight of everything I was feeling—

"You'll be the death of me... Quinn." My words were a fragile bridge spanning the vast ocean of emotions threatening to drown me, a whispered confession.

His eyes held a teasing glint as he smirked. "Escorts can't fall in love?"

"Who said anything about love?" I retorted, feigning nonchalance. But deep down, fear gripped me. I was dancing on the precipice, ready to fall, and I knew it.

"No one..." Quinn whispered, his gaze never leaving mine, tracing my every emotion, every guarded secret.

In the soft glow of the room, as stars twinkled outside, I placed the cowboy hat back on the bedside table, as I continued to trace infinity loops on his skin, each one echoing the vulnerability and uncertainty I felt. Terrified, yet inexplicably drawn to the warmth and honesty of the man beside me.

The familiar, comforting rhythm of Quinn's heartbeat against my ear juxtaposed sharply against the storm of thoughts swirling in my mind.

Deep-seated fears began to rise, uninvited, like shadows in the corners of my consciousness. Each one was an old wound, a memory of past betrayals and disappointments. Every laugh shared, every secret whispered, every moment of intimacy with past lovers—all had been tainted by eventual abandonment. They'd been charmed, intrigued, and eventually repelled by the very chaos that defined me—I had turned stone cold, for so long. A mask. A character. A vixen.

A tight knot of dread formed in my stomach. The thought of Quinn growing weary of my unpredictable ways, my erratic nature, was unbearable. I imagined him rolling his eyes one day, finding my quirks less endearing and more tedious. I envisioned the spark in his eyes dimming, replaced by that all-too-familiar look of annoyance and eventual indifference. The mere idea sent a sharp pang of fear through me.

Biting my lip, I pulled away slightly, gazing deep into his eyes. Those oceanic depths, for now, showed nothing but sincerity and warmth. But what if, one day, they mirrored the coldness I had seen in so many others?

As the silence stretched between us, a haunting whisper of doubt clouded my mind: What if I became just another chapter in his story, a fleeting memory eventually overshadowed by new adventures and lovers?

I shook my head subtly, willing the dark thoughts away. Tonight, in this ethereal cocoon we'd woven together, everything felt perfect. But lurking in the shadows was the chilling spectre of reality, waiting to test the strength of our newfound connection. The chapter of 'Vixen and Quinn' had just begun, and as much as I yearned for a fairy tale ending, I couldn't help but fear the twists and turns that awaited us.

♡ THROUGH THE ♡ LOOKING GLASS.

"It's not like I give a fuck"

The dim haze of backstage lights created a soft glow around my vanity, making me feel as though I was floating in a dream. It was in these quiet moments, legs up on my vanity, focused on the art of makeup, that I often lost myself in my thoughts. The brush strokes, the blending, the delicate application of eyeliner; all of it helped me forget. At least momentarily. But tonight, there was no escaping the relentless echo of Quinn's words; they resonated louder than the pulsating beats of club music beyond the walls.

"I have all the man I need."

Quinn's words, seemingly assuring at the time, now twisted my insides into anxious knots. Did he truly mean it? Or was it just one of those lines, said in the heat of the moment? I'd seen and heard it all. People often say things they don't mean, lost in the intoxication of passion.

And what about me? There was always that nagging voice in the back of my head, urging me to bolt before the heartache, to save myself the inevitable pain. It was the age-old dance I knew too well—when to stay, when to run.

Lollipop smack!

Kitty's heels clicked purposefully, announcing her arrival before I even saw her reflection next to mine in the mirror. "Sup, Dummy."

I forced a smirk. "Hey."

Her fingers started their familiar dance on my tense shoulders, her touch usually reassuring, but tonight, everything felt different. "Someone's in a mood."

I took a deep breath, steadying myself, drawing on every ounce of self-control to not let these doubts drown me in front of Kitty.

I kept my eyes focused on my reflection, avoiding a direct answer. "You heard from Aspen?" I mumbled, more to the mirror than her.

She paused, letting out a heavy sigh. "He's not doing too well…"

My hand quivered, smudging the almost-perfect line.

Damn it.

I cursed under my breath. Despite my efforts to dodge, she thrust the issue back at me, "and with Angel getting fired…" Kitty sighed. "It's just hard for everyone…" looking deep into my eyes, "Aspen would've lashed out at anyone, if they'd be reeling in his clients."

Lollipop smack!

Her attempt at comfort was lost on me, only feeding the fire within. I glanced at Kitty, my eyes drawn to that ever-present lollipop she always seemed to have. At times, I found it endearing, a sweet quirk of hers. But tonight, I viewed it differently. Was it her crutch? Did she use it to soothe herself, a sugary distraction from the night?

Suddenly, I felt a rush of insight, or perhaps just a—vicious deep-rooted—paranoia, tracing patterns where none existed. The lollipop—was it an act of infantilization on her part? An attempt to cling to the innocence we had all lost a long time ago? Or maybe she used it to appear more vulnerable, to attract a certain kind of clientele. In our line of work, projecting certain images could be lucrative.

In the thick of my tumultuous emotions, every little detail seemed magnified. I felt like I was in the centre of a universe where every gesture, every word was a veiled attack against me. That sense of impending doom, that something or someone was about to betray me, became overpowering.

Quinn, with his honeyed words and potentially vacuous promises, always kept me guessing, tugging at the fragile strings of my heart. Angel loomed like a storm cloud, her menacing threats promising to obliterate any semblance of peace. Emma Royd, the puppet master, played her part well, doling out cash in an attempt to disguise her shallow pretence of motherhood. And now Kitty, artfully wielding her child-like vulnerability like a weapon, casting me as the conniving antagonist in Aspen's tale. In the midst of this maelstrom, it became increasingly hard to discern the real from the feigned, the genuine allies from those who wore masks of friendship.

Enough.

And that's when the age-old defence mechanism kicked in—if I pushed everyone away first, they wouldn't have the chance to hurt me. Everyone was a threat; everyone was the enemy, even Kitty with her damn lollipop.

"You know," I spat, voice dripping with sarcasm, "maybe we should all just start carrying around lollipops, huh? Remind the world of the lost children we all are, parading in these grown-up bodies."

Kitty's eyes widened, clearly taken aback. But I wasn't done. The dam had broken, and a torrent of emotions, accusations, and insecurities poured out. I didn't want to wait for the blade to drop; I'd swing it myself.

Before I knew it, I was blurting out my defences. "Whatever... it's not like I give a fuck about anyone here anyways."

Lollipop smack!

She stopped massaging, the weight of her stare making my skin crawl. "That's a little harsh," she said, her voice edged.

I hardened my gaze on the mirror, never meeting her eyes. "It's just a job, Kitty."

Her eyes, filled with a mix of hurt and defiance, met mine in the mirror. "Well... what about me?"

"Oh, Hun," I replied, voice dripping with mock sweetness. "You're sweet, but so naive sometimes. That's the escort life. It's just what we do. Nothing personal."

The intensity of her gaze didn't waver. Refocusing on the smudged eyeliner, I tried to regain control of the conversation. "We hang around for a bit. Laugh. Drink. And move on."

The temptation to escape the tension was too great. Without much thought, I popped a pink pill, seeking the brief respite it promised. Craving the numbness it would bring. "It's a lone wolf's game," I whispered, mostly to myself.

Lollipop smack!

The weight in the room felt unbearable. Her lollipop moved aggressively in her mouth, and I couldn't help but apply my lipgloss in agitation. In this mirrored world, our unsaid words and emotions created a silent symphony, echoing the fractured reality of our lives.

Foot tapping. My knuckles cracking. *Lollipop smack!*

The ambiance of Jacqueline's shifted, like the sudden change in light when a cloud passes the sun. I noticed the telltale shimmer in the periphery of my vision, indicating the beginning of a daydream.

The room was suddenly awash in a disorienting red hue, neon lights casting an unsettling, bloody shade on everything. My surroundings seemed to pulsate, alternating between slow-motion languor and frenetic acceleration, mimicking the storm of emotions brewing within me. Out of nowhere, a vice-like grip clasped the nape of my neck, choking every rational thought. The next instant, my face was violently smashed against the vanity mirror, the world fragmenting as the glass splintered into a million pieces.

"You narcissistic piece of SHIT!" Kitty's voice sounded, not so much like her usual playful tone but like the raspy snarl of a wounded animal, her words dripping with a venom I'd never witnessed before.

Amidst the scattering shards, which felt like icy rain against my skin, sharp fragments embedded themselves in my cheeks. But the sting was nothing compared to the cold dread I felt when Kitty, eyes possessed by rage, picked up a dagger-like piece of the shattered mirror, its pointed end threateningly close to my exposed jugular.

Her cries pierced the heavy atmosphere, eerily distorted, a nightmarish blend of fury and despair. "AAAAAHHHH!"

Like a series of short-lived stars, the vanity bulbs began to falter under the sheer emotional voltage of the moment. One after another, they gave out, punctuating their exits with bursts of errant sparks, their brilliance snuffed out too soon, much like the fragile harmony that once existed between us.

Lollipop chomp!

Air caught in my throat as the surrealism of the red neon daydream shattered with the biting snap of a lollipop. My vision slowly recalibrated, the stark contrast between the menacing red haze and the blindingly bright backstage lights making everything momentarily blur. My ears refocused too, attuning themselves back to the familiar hum of Jacqueline's. When my vision settled, I stole a glance in Kitty's direction, I was taken aback.

Gone was the vulnerable, almost ethereal image of the girl who navigated the world with the delicate tread of a fawn. In her place stood a tempest, an embodiment of raw anger. Her eyes, usually shimmering with admiration or child-like wonder, now burned with a fire I had never witnessed before. This wasn't just fury; this was a culmination, an explosive end result of countless moments of being overlooked, underestimated, and pushed around.

The usually fragile curves of her face had sharpened, and the gentle lilt of her voice was replaced by a grounded, chilling silence. It was the silence of someone who'd been pushed past their breaking point. It was the type of fury born not just from the immediate confrontation, but from years of suppressed rage and indignation.

This was Kitty, not as the world saw her or wanted her to be, the immature child, but as she truly was—a powerhouse of a woman, a force of nature, demanding respect and space, no longer content being relegated to the shadows.

"It's no wonder you're always alone," she spat, her voice dripping with disdain. With a practiced flick of her wrist, she tossed the stick of her lollipop into a bin, never breaking eye contact. "All you do is push everyone away."

Her words were like daggers, and the direct hit caused me to flinch internally, even if my face remained stoic. The ice-cold reality of her statement left me in a transient daze, an eerie echo of the truths I'd danced around. The pain in her eyes, was a reflection of the pain I'd inflicted, not just on her, but on everyone who dared get close to me.

"You've got a client in room six," she muttered, the coldness in her voice matching the chill in the room. As she made her exit, a blast of the intense stage lights highlighted her silhouette, a momentary goddess amidst the divine chaos. For a split second, the glisten of a tear caught my eye before she blinked it away, shutting me out with her departure.

I felt an unfamiliar knot in my stomach—regret. Guilt. The knowledge that, deep down, I was the architect of my own loneliness. I'd sabotaged my chances at genuine connections, always hiding behind the facade of the confident, self-assured escort. But the real me? That person was terrified, always fearing rejection, betrayal.

How many times had I pushed people away? Built walls to keep myself safe? But from what? Love? Connection? Intimacy?

I don't fucking need those.

The reflection staring back at me in the vanity was a stranger. I'd grown so accustomed to burying my true feelings that I'd started to believe the lies I told myself. In that moment, the weight of my emotions felt like an anchor, dragging me down into uncharted depths.

My mask cannot crack.

I turned back to the mirror, facing the man that so many sought, yet so few truly knew. Forcing a smile that never quite reached my eyes, I whispered to myself, "Showtime."

♡ UNINVITED SHADOWS. ♡

"I'll gut him like a fucking fish"

The backstage corridors of Jacqueline's seemed endless and oppressively narrow tonight, as the intense confrontation with Kitty still echoed in my mind, her piercing words lingering like a bitter aftertaste.

I had to snap out of it, switch gears, and put on the Vixen facade. Clients didn't pay for emotional baggage, after all.

Breathing deeply, I tried to shake off the remnants of that emotionally charged encounter, mentally prepping my rehearsed lines and birth chart calculations, shuffling my tarot cards, ready to captivate another client—ready to weave another spellbinding tale.

I swung the door open with more force than necessary, wanting to assert control over at least something. As I flipped the switch, the feeble light gradually unveiled the room's sole occupant.

There, lounging with a smugness that could only belong to one person—

"Jay?"

A cold shiver ran down my spine. Every ounce of confidence I walked in with was ripped away in a heartbeat. "You're on time for once," I tried to sound light, nonchalant, even. "How'd you know I work here?"

Jay's smirk widened as he held up his phone, showcasing that damning PrideMate geolocation pin. "Only ten feet away," he drawled, emphasizing every word.

I bit the inside of my cheek, cursing my own oversight.

"You always were more of a cat than a vixen, leaving traces behind," he teased.

Anger swelled within, but right then, the weight in my fur coat pocket yanked me back to reality. My hand instinctively slid over the envelope inside. The reminder of why Jay was really here—the money I owed him. The same money I had been so confident of settling for the last two weeks, thinking it would erase him from my life for good.

"Eight grand, in cash," I said, trying to keep my voice steady. But the quiver betrayed me.

His laughter was cruel, echoing around the room, making my skin crawl. "Where's the rest, Doll?"

I took a deep breath, trying to steady my racing heart. This moment—right here—was what all the scheming had been for. I had played this scene in my head countless times, rehearsed every line, every expression. All of the trinkets I'd stolen, every wallet I'd pocketed from unsuspecting clients, every ring I'd discreetly slipped off a finger; it was all leading up to this. A carefully executed plan.

"You know how things are, Jay," I began, my voice betraying a hint of desperation. "Times are tough, and I'm doing everything I can." I reached into my coat, grasping a glimmering gold watch and a few pricey rings. "I've got these—and more upstairs. Should cover the difference."

I held them out as a peace offering, the sheen of the valuables covered more than my looming debt. And Jay always had a knack for owning precious things.

But as I threw it at him, the gold glinting briefly before reaching his hand, his mocking laughter intensified, emphasizing his dominance.

"Still doesn't quite cover my 16k," he sneered.

A claustrophobic feeling descended upon me. "We agreed on ten—," I stammered, struggling to find my footing against this unexpected assault.

He moved closer, making me feel small, insignificant. Every step he took felt like the noose tightening around my neck. "Interest adds up, Doll," he whispered, his foul breath mingling with the stale air of the room.

A thin sheen of sweat formed on my forehead, my breathing became shallow, and my ears rang with a piercing, high-pitched whine.

The watches, rings, wallets—all the steps I'd taken to claw my way out of this hole seemed insignificant now, like throwing pebbles into an abyss, hoping to fill it up.

I tried to muster some semblance of courage, a laugh slipping from my lips. But it was brittle, filled with fear. "No—No… no, no, NO! I'm not doing this again, Jay. You ALWAYS do this. You fucking LIAR. WE SAID TEN THOUSAND. I DON'T HAVE—"

His fingers were suddenly on my chin, forcing me to meet his cold gaze. "You'll figure it out. I'm giving you another chance."

A chance?

The word sounded grotesque coming from his lips. "YOU THINK THIS IS A CHANCE?!" I couldn't hold back my laughter, a manic, hopeless sound. And then, eyes widening, it dawned on me, something clicked—

"All you ever do is suffocate me," I murmured, my voice trembling. "I'll never be free. You just want to control me—"

"And about the company you keep..." Hiding under his poorly maintained leather jacket, with calculated cruelty, he pulled out: The cowboy hat.

Quinn's cowboy hat.

My heart raced, memories flashing before me.

Jay dropped the cowboy hat to his feet, a challenge in his eyes. His taunting voice was barely a whisper in my ear. "Oops. Why don't you pick that up for me... Doll."

But I couldn't back down, not now. I locked eyes with him, my glare filled with a desperation and defiance.

But it wasn't the hat that rattled me—it was the memory it invoked, the connection Jay was forging between me and Quinn.

I crouched, but not out of obedience. My defiance was palpable, a silent stand against the man who had once meant everything to me.

Jay's taunting smile widened. "Quinn? Was it? Handsome… but we can't have him around now, can we."

Every word dripped with malice, and for a moment, my resolve wavered. "Leave him out of this, Jay. I swear to FUCKING GOD!" I bellowed.

In that suffocating silence, I wrestled with the growing panic threatening to consume me. My mind raced, seeking a way out. A compromise. Anything. "Come on, Jay—Let's just… make it 12k… okay?" I tried to touch a part of him that was still human, rubbing his shoulder, hoping to find a glimmer of the man I once knew. "Just twelve, Hun. And then you leave us alone—"

His eyes widened, "Us?!"

That fucking us.

The world collapsed in a blur of rage and force. His fingers bit into my throat, slamming me against the wall. His threats echoed, the final nails in the coffin of our past. The cold wall pressed against my back as Jay's vice grip choked off my air supply. Panic bubbled inside of me, eyes darting around the dim room, searching for any way out.

"I'LL GUT HIM LIKE A FUCKING FISH—DO YOU HEAR ME, BITCH?!" Jay's threat, combined with his eyes that danced with madness, promised a depth of violence I had only ever seen once before. One time where I understood his threats weren't just empty promises of violent nature.

My vision blurred, the lack of air making my mind race. Through strained eyes, I could see Jay's lips move, taunting me further, "He doesn't get you like I do. You can't live without me, DOLL."

I felt the dark embrace of unconsciousness, its edges creeping into my vision. My chest screamed for air, my eyes watering from both pain and the suffocating despair of the situation.

"It's you and I. Till the end." And as if to seal my fate, Jay pressed his lips to mine, a perverse, possessive gesture.

The room dimmed, but just when hope seemed lost, the life-saving sound I hadn't dared hope for: the unmistakable click of a gun's chamber being adjusted by a glamour-toad of a drag queen.

And suddenly, Emma Royd's voice, firm and unyielding, rang out, "You best get outta here, Sugar." She aimed the pistol right between Jay's eyes, "I don't play well with strangers."

Jay released his grip, for all his bravado, knew when he was outmatched. "I better see that 16k by the end of the week—or you're fucking dead." With a parting threat and spit of disdain, he made his exit, leaving me trembling in the room's muted light.

His threat still hanging in the air, but I hardly cared. My attention was on the woman who had just saved my life.

"Ma—" I croaked, my voice raspy and raw from Jay's assault.

"Upstairs. NOW." Emma Royd was in no mood for talk.

My legs felt like lead, but I obeyed, leaving behind the room that had become a crucible for my past and present demons.

As I turned, walking through that door, the weight of our intertwined pasts bore down upon me. And Jay's shadow, a suffocating presence, clung to my every step.

♡ BALESTRA ♡

CHECKMATE.

"You're a selfish fuck, Vixen"

The door slammed shut behind me as I stormed into Emma's office, my heart pounding out a tribal beat in my chest.

"It's not as bad as—" I started.

"Who the hell was that?" Emma's voice was steel, the kind of steel that had seen years of bending but never breaking. "I'm not gonna put my girls in danger cause you can't keep good company, Vixen."

She yanked off her wig and tossed it onto the table, with an air of finality. Digging into her bra, she pulled out a cigarette and lit it. The room filled with the acrid smell of tobacco, masking the usual scent of perfume and desperation.

Cigarette crackle!

"You're out," she snapped.

No… no, no, no—

The words hit like a punch to the gut. PrideMate was no longer an option; Jay would have his eyes on it, waiting for a chance to pounce. My debt to him was more than just monetary—it was a noose around my neck, tightening with each desperate breath. "What? Come on, Mama. I need this gig. I can't go back on the streets—"

Images flashed before my eyes: Bambi's innocent face, our shared laughter, the little moments that made everything bearable. Jay's cruel intentions were clear—he wasn't just after me. He'd go for Bambi, too, my only solace in this twisted world. The thought sent waves of nausea rolling through me.

I tried to steady my breathing. There had to be a way out of this. But with each passing second, the weight of my predicament bore down on me. Desperation gnawed at the edges of my mind; if I lost this gig, the streets would claim me, and Jay would have exactly what he wanted: complete and utter control. The walls of my world were closing in, and I felt trapped.

I had to think. I had to find a way out, not just for me, but for Bambi.

The fear must have shown on my face, because she paused for a moment, her eyes softening, just slightly.

"He'll fucking kill me!" I couldn't help the panic seeping into my voice.

Cigarette crackle!

She inhaled her cancer stick, sweating profusely. "Not my problem anymore." Taking a drag, she paused and exhaled, leaving a smoky cloud between us. "Look at what you've done, Vixen. Ya broke everyone in this goddamn house..." She coughed up a lung. "I had to give Aspen a loan—Kitty just bolted outta thin air—and Angel... for Chrissakes..."

I followed her glare to my vanity, my heart sinking as she yanked the drawer open, revealing the stash I had hoped would remain hidden. "And what about this? This is how you repay me? Stealing from clients?" She dangled a ruby encrusted ring. "I've backed your shit up. Chance after chance—when everyone was gunnin' for ya

—and now Aspen tells me you've been swiping these from clients. Behind my back?"

That fucking rat.

"Little snitch," I muttered under my breath.

"You know how much shit I'm in because of you? Stealin' from clients—unbelievable." Emma pulled out another one of her cigarettes, desperately trying to calm herself down. "Angel was right about you." Her voice was rising now, her disappointment giving way to anger.

Cigarette crackle!

The cigarette, always perched precariously between Emma Royd's fingers or lips, was more than just a vice—it was her talisman. Each stick, slender and white, symbolized the battles she had faced, the myriad storms she had weathered. Its ethereal smoke held whispered secrets of the brothel, and its glowing ember mirrored the fire in her spirit. To many, it was just another toxin, but to Emma, it was a lifeline, an ever-present companion through life's darkest alleys. The very alleys she'd known for years—and fought to stay out of.

"You're a selfish fuck, Vixen," she spat, her words dripping with disdain. "Get out."

"Please—" I was begging now, my voice a pathetic whine.

But she was done. "OUT! NOW!"

She shooed me out of her office, each word sent me stumbling back out into the narrow hallway. The walls seemed to lean in closer, as if they too were turning their backs on me.

My head was spinning as I made my way down the corridor, Emma's words reverberating in my mind. Selfish. Out. Kill. I was a pariah, an outcast even among outcasts. Jay had seen to that.

His threats, his sickening ownership of me—it all loomed larger now that I had lost my sanctuary. The anger and fear intermingled, boiling up within me until I thought I would burst.

He said it would be just the two of us, till the end. A twisted forever that I wanted no part of.

And Emma—she had been my last chance, my only haven in a world that had always been more battlefield than home. But now, even that was gone. She had pushed me out, into the dark, into the den of wolves.

I reached the exit, my hand trembling as it gripped the door handle. It felt like a threshold, a line in the sand beyond which there could be no return. With a deep breath, I stepped out into the night, each footstep a leap into an uncertain abyss, onto the dark, wet, parking lot.

My heels clicked against the wet asphalt as I stood under the dim glow of the flickering lamppost, under pouring rain. A pathetic fallacy if any.

The door behind me burst open and bags of my belongings came tumbling out into the rain-soaked night. Clothes, makeup, little trinkets I had collected—each item a piece of the life I had built here.

Emma stood there, clutching one last bag, her eyes meeting mine for a split second…

The dim light accentuated the deep creases on her face, every wrinkle a testament to the life she had lived, a life not much different from mine. For a fleeting moment, her hardened gaze softened, and there it was—a silent communication between us. Her eyes echoed a thousand unsaid words: "I know, Vixen. I know the cruelty of the streets, the shadows that lurk and the hands that snatch. Believe me, I've walked those dark alleys too."

A hint of maternal warmth, usually so well concealed, surfaced in her eyes. It was the look of a mother forced to abandon her child for the sake of the many. "It's you or my girls," they seemed to say.

That split-second exchange was like a dance between two souls that had faced the same battles, suffered the same wounds. Emma's face became a canvas of her own story, mirrored in my own experiences.

Then, breaking the palpable tension between us, she whispered, "I'm sorry." A cruel irony that would be etched in my memory forever.

Her voice softer now, carrying a weight of finality. "Good luck, Sugar."

With that, she tossed the final bag into the puddle forming at my feet, sending my belongings scattering in all directions. The door slammed shut behind her, echoing in the empty parking lot.

My heart ached as I gathered my scattered life. The rain washed over me, smearing my makeup, soaking my clothes. Amongst the debris, my eye caught the sheen of my scandalous red rhinestone thong, discarded like a fallen warrior.

As my fingers brushed against the wet fabric of the red rhinestone thong, a rush of memories overwhelmed me. Before Jacqueline's, before the backstage banter and the makeup-streaked tears, before it all—that thong was my armour.

I shoved it into the bag, my hands trembling, and looked around at my scattered belongings, at the closed door behind me, at the desolate parking lot stretching out in front of me, and I realized—I was free. Terrifyingly, horribly free.

I was out, but I couldn't let myself come down. I couldn't afford to. There was a price to pay. A debt to clear. And lives to save. The game wasn't over.

And in this game, I wasn't just a pawn. I was the king.

And it was my move.

♡ PRIDEMATE. ♡

My heart thrummed a frantic beat, as I stormed into my loft. But before the door could even slam behind me, Quinn, ever the beacon of cheer, was already chirping from the stove. "Hello, Dolly. I tried calling, but mister big-shot was too busy. Another grand soirée?"

"I got fired," I spat out, my voice tinged with a volatile mixture of bitterness and humiliation. I headed straight for my personal bar, where I poured myself a generous glass of gin.

"We'll find you a new job," Quinn suggested, trying to remain upbeat. But his optimism only heightened my irritation.

I chuckled sarcastically, the sound more of a growl as I reached for my MDMA baggy. It was empty. "Of course," I muttered to myself, not at all surprised by my latest misfortune.

I took a sip of gin, hoping the liquid courage would dampen the chaos swirling inside me. Quinn tried again. "I'm sure they're hiring at some bar—"

Fuck right off.

"Yeah? And what do I scribble under 'past experiences', Quinn?" I retorted, pacing back and forth. My eyes caught sight of Quinn's handwriting on the heart-shaped nipple cover plastered to the fractured window. "Do I just tell them my only experience ever is fucking escorting, Quinn?" Another sip of gin fortified my words. "That I've been a runaway my whole life? That I steal? And what happens when they find out about my pimp? Or the drugs?"

In a fit of anger, I tossed the empty MDMA baggy across the room, and it hit the wall with a soft, almost laughable thud.

"I'm not like you," I snarled. "I can't just get a normal job. Not everyone has it easy or simple, Quinn."

Laughing bitterly, I theatrically raised my hand and bowed. "Right. The fucking hurricane, ladies and gentlemen."

Quinn moved closer, his face softening, a conciliatory gesture. "Dance with me—"

Those words, which once seemed so endearing, filled with promise and an escape from reality, now stung like an ill-timed jest. I'd always admired his ability to find positivity, to dance through the storm. But this time, it felt like a pointed disregard for my feelings—a blithe attempt to mask the rawness of the moment with a waltz. It was as if he was suggesting that a few twirls and steps could magically erase the mess outside the rhythm of the music.

"NO! WHAT THE FUCK?" I yelled, cutting him off, my voice tinged with disbelief and outrage.

"Vixen, I'll help you. It'll be fine," Quinn's voice was tender, but I could detect the restraint, his eyes pleading for a break, like he was treading on a minefield, where any wrong step would trigger an explosion.

"Fine? You think this is fine?!" I glared at him, taking deep breaths to steady my racing heart. I swallowed hard, my throat dry from the gin and the raw emotions bubbling up. Quinn's goodwill couldn't touch me now; it couldn't penetrate the fortress of anger and self-pity I had built around myself.

In this dark moment, under the harsh lighting of my own skewed reality, even love—or what felt like it—

seemed like a mirage. A false oasis in a desert I had created myself.

And so I threw back the gin, letting it burn its way down. It wasn't just about the alcohol. I was swallowing down years of hurt, defiance, and mistrust. Not just the gin, but also my chances at something real, something different. It's easier to stick with the devil you know, and for now, that was enough.

I was breathing heavily, fists clenched so tight my knuckles were white. "What do you want?" I snapped at Quinn.

"You. I want you," he answered softly, reaching out to take my drink away. "Can you stop with that, please? Let's just talk—"

"What the fuck do you want with me?!" I yelled, gulping down another sip of gin.

A powerful wave of emotion surged from the depths of my soul. My vision became momentarily blurred, not by tears, but by a flood of memories and feelings threatening to break free.

"I'm just another pretty thing to play with, is that it? Like every other fucking pervert! Just a thing to use up, and throw away when you're done with it? Huh?"

The question hung in the air like an impending storm, and I couldn't stop the words from tumbling out. "Or are you the type who wants to fix me? Does it make you feel good about yourself? Powerful? Which fucking kink am I to you, Quinn? Is it the doll or fixing the whore?"

My chest tightened, and my eyes welled up as I gulped down the oversized shot of gin. I looked at him, my vision blurred. "Well, I'm not fucking broken!"

With that, I threw my glass with all the force I could muster. It shattered against the window, perfectly hitting the sharpied **Hello, Dolly. See you tonight!** on the nipple cover.

Quinn sighed, his expression unreadable, as I muttered "Get out."

He seemed to debate whether to argue or comply. Finally, steadying himself on the bar, he spoke, "Come on, Vix—"

"I don't need you. Get out," I interrupted, the neon sign above us screeching as if echoing my inner turmoil.

Quinn hesitated, then drew closer.

There was a split second where my inner voice, that faint whisper of reason, begged me to restrain myself, to not say things I'd regret. But the tidal wave was too strong, drowning that rational plea. Words formed at the tip of my tongue, laced with venom, a culmination of years of pent-up feelings and abandonment issues. Even as they began to spill out, I could feel a pang of immediate regret, a sinking sensation in the pit of my stomach. But it was too late to take them back. And I uttered the final jab—

"It was always just another gig, anyway."

After the biting words left my mouth, I saw a shift in Quinn's demeanour. It was subtle, a mere flicker of hurt in those normally steady eyes. For a moment, pain seemed to seep through the cracks. An immense—gut-wrenching pain.

His chest moved slightly, taking in a deep breath, steadying himself. Where I was tempestuous and wild, he was the picture of calm. My eyes darted over his face, noting the way he withheld his pain, keeping it locked away.

It was almost infuriating how composed he remained. I was chaos incarnate, a tempest of emotions crashing and burning around me. But Quinn? Quinn was the ever-steady flame, unwavering in the harshest of winds.

He knew how to act. He knew how to listen. He knew how to love. He never matched my anger or rose to my provocations, always staying calm, always the rock. In this moment, as in so many others, Quinn was the radiant sun—

Warm, unwavering, shining steadily even as clouds sought to obscure his light. He had a way of loving, of listening, a maturity that I hadn't yet mastered. And as much as it pained me to admit it, I envied him for it.

Quinn pulled back, a jolt of surprise emanating from his eyes, his mouth agape—once, twice—as if he was grappling with the whirlwind of words I'd thrown his way. "They can look. They can touch… but you'll never let them in, eh?"

I was rooted to the spot, the weight of my rash outburst pinning me down. His voice grew softer, yet more piercing, "always running away first… you know, true passion, true connection, isn't about who you let touch you. It's when intimacy surpasses the boundaries of the physical—That's when you know you've truly loved."

A tremor passed through my lips, a crack in the dam of my resolve.

"I wish you could've seen what I saw, you know," he murmured, a wistful sadness lingering in his voice. "The real you. The vulnerability. The intimacy. The guy I fell for on the dance floor… maybe revisit that place inside your mind someday, and who knows…" he paused, staring into my eyes as if it were a final goodbye, and let out, "you might still find us dancing."

Ping!

PrideMate.

Quinn sighed, then smiled. "Better not keep them waiting," he said, slinging his bag over his shoulder and walking out the door. As—

I stood there, alone. Paralyzed.

Ping!

He actually walked out—

Ping!

As that ping echoed in the room, every atom in me resonated with a blend of loathing and despair. In that precise moment, it wasn't just a notification; it was a mocking siren, a bitter reminder of how PrideMate had corrupted my essence. The damn app, with its endless carousel of faces and hollow promises, had insidiously wormed its way into my psyche, turning me into this... monster. This detached, toxic escort who believed in the ephemeral over the eternal, the superficial over the profound.

Once, I had been someone who danced with abandon, who could find intimacy in a single, prolonged gaze. Now, my soul had been tainted, commoditized by the countless swipes and faceless conversations. Quinn had been the counterbalance to that world, a tether to reality and genuine emotion. And I had just let him walk away.

My fingers gripped the phone, the cold device suddenly feeling like a chain binding me to a world I no longer recognized. The weight of regret, resentment, and realization culminated into a furious energy.

My lip trembling, tears streaming down my face, and with a scream, I flung the device, trying to sever the chains that PrideMate had wrapped around me. "SHUT THE FUCK UP!"

But even as it crashed, I knew that the real battle was against the demons the app had nurtured within me.

Ping!

Another PrideMate ping filled the silence, mocking me. But it was the silence that followed—the haunting emptiness—that hurt the most.

And in that moment, amid the shattered glass and broken illusions, I realized how terrifyingly loud that silence could be, but it was the faint memory of the **Death** card pulled prior that seemed to haunt me the most.

♡ RUN, BOY, RUN. ♡

"The show must go on"

The cacophony of that rickety-ass gym dominated the atmosphere—treadmills whirring, weight plates clanging, and the occasional obnoxious grunt punctuating the air. I pushed the speed up another notch, the display flashing: **7.5...8.0...8.5 mph.**

Enter Mr. Overcompensating—some buffed up, balding from steroids, thirty-or-so-year-old who dared to approach me. "How long you got, Bro—"

"Fuck off creatine dumpster," I snapped.

He glared me down, confused. Barely comprehending what had just happened. And walked away.

Lost in the repetitive rhythm of the treadmill, my mind began to drift, pulled back by the tide of last night's memories. "You might still find us dancing," he'd whispered.

That phrase looped in my head, a dance of its own. The promise of a dance not just of bodies, but of souls. The idea of a future where our connection might lead us back to each other, back to a dance floor where our stories, with all their flaws and chaos, could intertwine. And for a fleeting moment amidst the gym's din, I could almost hear the soft hum of our song, feel the pull of our dance.

Quinn's chat screen on my phone was still open. **What a night, Dolly! See you tomorrow?... maybe?** He had written.

Just another gig, right?

I glanced around the gym. Dumbbells, oversized workout machines, gym bros checking themselves out in the mirror—none of it really mattered. I was on autopilot. Until—

My phone buzzed. The screen screaming at me.

INCOMING CALL FROM BAMBI

I hit the "decline" button, my thumb trembling slightly over the screen.

Nope.

It didn't matter. I turned up the speed again, my feet pounding the treadmill in sync with the thud of my heart. The speed display flashed: **9.0...9.5 mph.**

Quinn's words came rushing back to me: "Intimacy isn't about who you let touch you. It's about who you choose to give your attention when dozens of people are asking for it."

Intimacy was a luxury I couldn't afford.

Ping!

I felt my phone vibrate in the cup holder. My eyes grew wide.

Finally!

(PatStar1): **You do boyfriend experiences? 2 hours**

Not Quinn...

I paused, fingers hovering over the keyboard. A part of me wanted to ignore it. A part of me wanted to run, to keep running until my lungs gave out. Instead—

(Me): Of course, Hun! Where you taking me?

The words appeared on the screen, as if willing themselves into existence. I sent the message.

For a moment, I considered what I'd just done. Was this really it? Just gonna go back to my ways? Another gig, another dance—a life stuck in perpetual motion but never truly moving forward.

With a heavy sigh, I shut off my phone and pushed the speed up on the treadmill once more. The display flashed: **10.0 mph**. My feet pounded the rotating belt, a relentless rhythm that drowned out everything else.

I wasn't just running on the treadmill. I was running from myself, from Quinn, from Bambi, from everything that had the potential to touch me deeper than skin level.

And the irony of it all? The faster I ran, the more I felt like I was standing still.

In the flashing neon heart of Suite 701, I found myself again. Different night, different arms holding me close— arms that were looking for a "two hour boyfriend experience" nonetheless. A mood I was less than interested in.

The music pulsed through the air like an electric current, charging the atmosphere with a sense of reckless abandon. But for me, the lights were a little too bright, the music a little too loud. A little too reminiscent of a time when these walls felt like home.

I was out of my element—or rather, uncomfortably in it—dancing awkwardly through a world I was losing my grip over. Everywhere I looked, memories of Quinn seemed to lurk, waiting to drag me back to a time when I had danced these floors without a care.

Patrick was all too chipper, clearly eager for his "two-hour boyfriend experience." A stout ginger bearded daddy, whose idea of a good time was ironically similar to my idea of purgatory.

"You sure about this place? Their drinks are… um, weak as fuck," I shouted over the blaring music, almost as an excuse.

"What? Music's great!" Patrick replied, his eyes lighting up, "you've ever been here?"

My eyes caught a young couple on the dance floor, their arms wrapped tightly around each other. "Yeah," I muttered, feeling a twinge of something I couldn't quite put a finger on.

Spotting two unattended cocktails at the bar, I grabbed them, downing the first one in one gulp. "Once upon a dream. Or…" I winced at the taste, "however it fucking goes in Beauty and the Beast."

Patrick looked confused. "You mean Sleeping Beauty?"

I shot him a look that would have made Medusa proud, forcing a smile. "You're a Virgo, right?"

Bewildered, he nodded. "Yeah! How'd you—"

"It shows," I interrupted, clutching my second cocktail like it was my lifeline. He was missing the point, but then again, most people do.

Patrick eyed my second cocktail for an instant, before realizing I would never dare share, and wobbled off to the bar. "Uh, guess I'll go grab myself one."

As he walked away, my phone buzzed—

INCOMING CALL FROM BAMBI

Declining it, I threw back my remaining cocktail, and popped a pink pill from my pocket. The pulsating beats felt momentarily distant, overtaken by the unmistakable prickling sensation of being observed.

Over by the bar stood a man, head shaven clean, drink clutched tightly in hand, his eyes raking over me with hunger. A few tables away, a woman in a smoky-eyed makeup and a blazing red dress shot me a predatory glance, her lips parting as if savouring a forbidden thought. And then there was the couple tucked away in a shadowy corner, their hushed exchanges briefly interrupted as their combined gaze fixed on me, exchanging sly smiles of shared fantasies.

These gazes weren't simple glances of admiration or fleeting interest. They bore into me, stripping me of layers, wanting, possessing. Eyes that saw not the person but an object—an alluring commodity, a tantalizing trophy.

A surge of anger and revulsion bubbled up within me. These strangers, with their ravenous eyes, saw just the facade, just the allure. They were blind to the soul beneath, the heart filled with emotions, dreams, and vulnerabilities. To them, I was nothing more than an object of fascination, a morsel of fantasy. That's all I had ever been. And I hated that. I hated them—I hated them all.

As the euphoria began to seep its way through my system, I knew that I was on a path I couldn't easily turn back from. But tonight, I didn't care. I just wanted to feel something—even if it wasn't real.

I caught a glimpse of myself in the mirrored wall. The disheveled hair, the overly dilated pupils. It was like seeing a ghost—one who looked trapped. Desperate.

My eyes landed on a half-empty bottle of champagne sitting forlornly on another table. I grabbed it and chugged what was left, as if trying to fill the emptiness inside me with its bubbling contents.

The effects of the pink pill were beginning to kick in, adding a layer of unreality to an already surreal night. As the world around me started to swirl, I felt a buzz in my pocket. My phone again.

It was another call from Bambi. I stared at the screen for what felt like an eternity. Finally, I declined the call.

Amid the glaring lights and blaring music, a primal urge clawed at the back of my mind—a relentless urge to run. Flee. Escape from this cage of neon and noise. It was instinctual, the very marrow of my bones screaming at me to bolt. To find the nearest exit and vanish into the night.

Every fibre of my being seemed attuned to that singular thought: Run, Vixen, run! The way out of any predicament, any emotional entanglement, any mistake was always to run. It was how I dealt with vulnerability, with pain, with anything too raw or real. A defence mechanism perfected over years, a trusty escape hatch I could always rely on.

But where had that gotten me? Every hasty exit, every avoided confrontation, just added another chain, another layer of walls around me.

I wasn't done running, but I didn't know where to go.

For a moment, I felt truly lost. The weight of my past, my choices, my mistakes, bearing down on me all at once.

Then the DJ transitioned to a new track, a song I remembered from what felt like a lifetime ago. As the familiar melody filled the air, something inside me twitched.

Maybe it was the music, maybe it was the champagne, or maybe it was hitting rock bottom, but something was off—

That's when it happened. The table seemed to come out of nowhere. Or maybe I was just too out of it to notice. Either way, I stumbled, crashing into it and sending its contents flying into a cloud of glass shards.

The crash silenced the room for a microsecond, all eyes turning towards me. I could see the judgment in their faces, the disdain.

"I'm fine, loves," I slurred, picking myself up and attempting to reclaim some semblance of dignity. "Go— the show must go on."

♡ THERE'S GOT TO BE ♡ A MORNING AFTER.

"No drinks. No drugs. NO clients"

Fucking sunlight.

The rays had poured in through my half-assed attempt at blinds, hitting my eyes like laser beams. Even the light seemed intrusive, judgmental, catching every dirty corner of my loft— the gin bottles, the discarded thongs, the leather harnesses. Each object was a little monument to the previous night's chaos, or perhaps, to a lifetime of it.

Tangled in my own mess on the couch, with makeup streaked like war paint, my mullet seemed to have partied harder than even I had remembered. The shimmering tattoos, inking stories from drunken nights and forgotten lovers, played hide and seek under the dappled sunlight. But the star of the show—of last night's debauchery—was the deepening bruise on my forearm, a purple memento of a fall I "couldn't"—or wouldn't—recall.

My head felt like it hosted a death metal concert, but just as I was sinking into self-pity, the universe decided I needed more—a series of knocks rattled through the room.

"Fuck off," I muttered, pulling the blanket over my head, but then the door slammed open.

Bambi. Of course.

He'd always had an untimely knack for, well, everything. Breaking my not-so-blissful hangover nap. His loud, unapologetic entrance was as jarring as the headache pounding in my skull.

Rise and shine, Bitch." Bambi barked, yanking the blanket off me.

I winced in pain. "No." My hangover intensifying at his audacity.

"You ignored my calls—Fine. Probably dancing, so no big deal," he went on, pulling a bottle of pain meds from his purse and tossing it at me. "But no follow-ups. No texts. No sign of life for DAYS—you freaking ghosted me.

When you literally have a price over your head. You are stressing me THE FUCK out, Vix—what's going on?!"

I couldn't bring myself to meet his eyes, instead focusing on the unbearable sunlight filtering through the curtains, hand pressed to my forehead.

"That hangover's gonna be a mess," Bambi sassily called out.

I grunted and sighed, annoyed more by the intervention than by the invasion of my privacy. "Not if I keep going."

And then he saw it—the bruises on my arm.

"What happened to your arm?" Bambi's voice shifted from annoyance to genuine concern.

"It's nothing," I replied, lying through my teeth as I poured gin into a martini glass. "Just a stupid accident."

His concern made my skin crawl. It was like looking into a mirror and hating what you see. And I did. I hated that I'd worried him, hated that I was causing someone else pain because I couldn't manage my own shit.

His eyes didn't leave my arm. "Vixen. Please—what's going on?"

"It's NOTHING—I'm FINE. I just—" I winced again, "went out last night and got a little too fucked... tripped and landed on a table. Really hard. OKAY? That's ALL."

"Okay," Bambi muttered.

"OKAY!" I shouted back, at my wits end.

The silence seemed to last for an eternity. Then, Bambi drew closer. "Did you give Jay the money?" he asked, finally stepping back a bit.

A pang of guilt hit me hard. There it was, the question I'd dreaded. Standing at the crossroads of truth and deception.

I could see the subtle wear on Bambi's face, the signs of sleepless nights and unwarranted stress. Perhaps a small lie, a temporary deceit, would buy me the time I needed to fix this mess. I'd find a way to get the money, pay Jay back, and keep Bambi shielded from the impending storm. I could handle Jay, or so I tried to convince myself.

I swallowed hard and nodded, avoiding his probing eyes. Bambi sighed, relieved. He hugged me from behind, and for a second, I almost let myself lean into it. Almost.

"Good. That's good." Bambi looked up, his eyes filled with tears. "I have a show Saturday. Out of town, so I won't be around for a few days…" He sighed. "Take a break, too, please?" he said, turning me around to face him. "No drinks. No drugs. NO clients."

For a moment, his eyes met mine, and I could see a flicker of hope. Like maybe, just maybe, if I said yes, everything would be okay between us. Between me and the world. Between me and myself.

I forced a smile and nodded, knowing damn well I wasn't promising anything.

"Good. Call me if you need anything. Love ya, babe," he said, and then he was gone, leaving me alone in the echoing emptiness of my loft, with nothing but the dying sunlight spotlighting my mess. Its exit leaving me trapped in the creeping dusk, imprisoned by the coming night.

I stood there, fidgeting with my nails, mouth opening and closing as if words would magically come out. Words that would explain everything: the bruises, the gin, the random hookups, the perpetual chaos that was my life.

But no words came. Bambi was out.

And so, I was left alone, suffocated by the silence and the unspoken words that seemed to scream at me, reminding me of who I was—or rather, who I had refused to leave behind.

The loft felt emptier than before, like a physical echo of what was going on inside me. But emptiness was a feeling I could understand, a feeling I could manage.

I took a deep breath and strode over to my red fur coat, searching for any hint of monetary salvation, and pulled out my wallet—empty.

Of course it was. The universe wasn't done with its little joke at my expense.

Grimacing, I turned to my last resort: PrideMate. I updated my headline to: **!LOOKING NOW$$**. Fingers tapping, eyes scanning, heart sinking. I waited.

Nothing.

No messages, no taps, no interest.

Frustrated, I took the initiative, shooting a message to **DOMTOP43.**

(Me): **Hey, Hun. Looking?$**

I smirked, a play of false confidence. And waited. When—

Ping!

(DOMTOP43): **Not a Sugar Daddy. See ya.**

My eyes rolled almost involuntarily. I tried another guy.

Ping!

(JJBtm): **Ew. no.**

Rejected.

And another.

Ping!

Rejected.

It was a string of digital doors slamming in my face, each echoing louder than the last.

There I was, staring at my empty wallet. I took a swig of gin straight from the bottle, the liquid fire burning less than my current life situation. Maybe a pink pill would do the trick, another leap into an artificial paradise. I popped one and felt its familiar yet deceitful comfort flood my system.

And then I rushed out, leaving behind the comfort of my loft, propelled by the desperation that seemed to be the only constant in my life.

Sunlight. Now a fading memory, as the darkness encroached. Embracing the night—rushing headlong into it.

♡ LOVE ME, ♡ PLEASE LOVE ME.

"You'll survive"

The red emergency lights of the bathhouse cast an otherworldly glow, creating a contorted path of obscurity and whispered promises. Everything was a blur. I could barely navigate through the winding maze of cubicles, where I could hear the faint and sketchy moans that were coming from inside the walls. Underground, grungy, the kind of place where the air would give you chlamydia—I was adrift in a gay sex-fuelled labyrinth that might as well have been the ninth circle of Hell.

I navigated the maze, my senses dulled and heightened in all the wrong ways. Men roamed in white towels, predatory and cautious, a dance of desire and detachment. Those same shadows seemed to dance and jeer at my desperate attempt to keep a grip on reality. This underworld, with its pungent aroma—a mix of musk, sweat, and a hint of regret—was where I had allowed my life to sink.

But I was there for something different—money, client, stability in the unstable world I had come to know. Leaning against the wall, prowling PrideMate.

Ping!

(RobTopXXL): **Room 332.**

A smirk crossed my lips. I strutted down the maze of narrow hallways and passed by Dante and Denver—two crusty-lipped twinks who looked like they had lived a few lifetimes too many. They snickered as I walked by, their mocking stare tracing every move I made. I rolled my eyes; I had no time for the spectators of my descent.

Eager, I made my way toward a bulky figure. "Rob! Hun!" I exclaimed, spinning him around, only to grimace at the stranger's face.

Wrong guy. FML.

The grim-reaper—shrivelled prune—looking stranger smirked at me, his eyes filled with a predatory kind of lust I wasn't desperate enough to entertain. Just then—

Ping!

(RobTopXXL): **Never mind. Found someone else.**

Hold the fuck up, Boomer.

My eyes widened in disbelief. I scanned the dimly lit hallway and spotted room 332. In a matter of seconds, I spotted my so-called 'client' with Denver, smugly entering the room, sealing the door—along with my hopes— behind them.

Every encounter mattered, every client was a lifeline. Losing Rob wasn't just about pride; it was about survival.

Fury ignited within me. I turned around and made a beeline toward Denver's acolyte—Dante. "What the HELL was that?" I demanded.

Dante raised an eyebrow, clearly amused. "Excuse me?"

"You know DAMN WELL what I'm talking about, Hun," I snarled. "You pimp out the guy who just walked into 332?" My fingers brushed against the textured wall, a strange tactile sensation that made me giggle. Maybe it was the pink pill. Maybe it was the gin. Maybe it was the sheer absurdity of it all.

"Denver?" Dante looked both bemused and slightly offended.

I was spiralling, caught in a storm of bad decisions, bitter confrontations, and a desperate need for something to go right. Each dismissal, each closed door pushed me further into the labyrinth. "You just poached my PrideMate client, Bitch." A heady mix of drugs, frustration, and the erratic rhythm of the bathhouse made my voice wobble between seductive and sardonic.

Dante broke into a sneer. He seemed amused, an infuriating smirk crossing his face as he told me how the world worked here. "This isn't PrideMate turf, sweetheart. This is a bathhouse."

"That's still no excuse to—"

A sudden touch brushed against my arm, interrupting my rant. My eyes rolled back for a moment, an involuntary reaction to whatever cocktail of substances was coursing through my veins.

Dante cut me off. "Entitled little PrideMate escorts, all the same. It's every bitch for themselves, you know? Nothing personal," he said, as if I were a child learning the rules of a cruel game.

I leaned against the wall, the texture again eliciting a soft moan from me. I felt like I was on the verge of unraveling.

"Go home, rookie," Dante sneered, "You'll survive," sauntering off like he owned the place.

I stared at Dante's retreating figure, swallowed whole by the labyrinthine darkness of the bathhouse. Each red-tinged corner felt like another layer of hell, another twist in a maze that offered no way out.

"Surviving, my ass," I muttered under my breath, disgusted at how trivial Dante made it sound. It wasn't mere survival; it was a frantic scramble for air as I drowned in my own life.

Ping!

Another PrideMate escapade. Mechanically, I pulled it out, stared at the screen, and then silenced it. I was high, so damn high, but not the good kind of high. This was the kind where reality bent and twisted until I was spiralling down a tunnel with no end.

I slid my phone back into my pocket, where it belonged, silenced and ignored. Just like me.

"Get a grip, Vix," I told myself. But how do you get a grip when the walls keep moving, when the floor under you feels like a vortex sucking you deeper into a pit?

I was at the edge, standing on a precipice built of my own poor choices, pharmaceutical assistance, and a hefty dose of despair. Each look from the men around me, each mocking laugh, every dismissive gesture shoved me closer to the edge.

My mind was an echo chamber of doubt, paranoia, and desperate need. A need for validation, for worth, for something to grasp onto before I completely unraveled.

I was supposed to be the lone wolf. Strong. Talented with seduction. Instead, here I was, falling apart in a bathhouse, unable to even secure a client.

"You're losing it," I thought. And the terrifying part was, I didn't know how to stop it. My usual answers—alcohol, pills, a quick trick—all seemed so irrelevant now. They were temporary solutions to an existential problem. They were band-aids for a soul-bleeding wound.

The red lights around me blurred as I blinked back tears I didn't know I had. This bathhouse. Dark corners, no exit, and a constant, cloying atmosphere that threatened to choke me—I was Alice, lost in Wonderland.

I knew I had to move, to walk out of this place, to find some air. But my feet felt rooted, my body heavy, my spirit crushed. So, I stood there, lost in a maze of damned souls, wondering if this was my destiny—to spiral forever in darkness, never finding my way out. Would I become Dante? Or Denver? Was this it?

The walls closed in. My options dwindled, evaporated, until they were as nonexistent as my will to fight. I was lost within the labyrinth, but even worse, I was lost within myself. And I didn't know if I would ever find my way out.

The glaring red lights seemed to penetrate my soul, exposing me for what I had become—a wreck, a cliche, a cautionary tale. Adrift in a sea of despair and yearning, chasing after connections as ephemeral as the smoky air.

Where was I going? What was I doing? Questions pounded in my head, each unanswered, as I stumbled further into the void. With each step, I sank deeper into the quagmire of my own making, utterly lost.

I was out of my depth, groping in the dark in a place where darkness reigned. I pressed my hand over my mouth to stifle a rising gag, my stomach revolting against the cocktail of emotions and substances. And there it was. My salvation:

A motherfucking urinal.

The harsh blue lights from the neon above glowed like a chilling aurora, casting an unsettling hue on the rundown urinal of the bathhouse. There it was, singular and mocking in its openness. It was as if it revelled in my humiliation. The words **Rest in Piss** adorned the wall in crude spray paint. A kind of sacrilege and irony all in one.

To absolutely no surprise at all, a man was sitting next to the urinal, wearing nothing but a BDSM mask designed for piss play—another soul lost in the catacombs of human desire and degradation. He looked up as I approached, his glistening eyes hidden behind the leather, eager, but I could feel them on me, knowing, waiting. For a moment, we were united in this underworld, our fates written in urine and leather.

But I wasn't there for some twisted desire of his.

I couldn't hold it back anymore.

I darted towards it, dropping my phone in the rush. My knees hit the cold tiles as I threw myself over the urinal. Violently, almost cathartically, I hurled into the porcelain vessel. Once, twice, until it felt like I had nothing left inside me, neither dignity nor despair.

I rested there for a moment, my forehead against the cold rim, wiping away the acidic residue from my mouth. I felt empty, like a shell stripped of its life. How did it come to this? Was this my rock bottom? Or was there a lower depth still to explore?

Ping!

PrideMate. Cutting through the stillness like a bullet. With a weary hand, I picked it up and read the message on the screen.

(Buttstuffr4): **You free for an hour?**

I hesitated. Another opportunity that could either lead to my further fall or offer a tenuous lifeline.

I looked at myself in the cracked mirror across from me, my eyes hollow, my face washed in the unforgiving blue light. What I saw was a wreck who had reached his limit but was still teetering on the edge, staring out the window and into the void.

With a shaky finger, I replied.

(Me): **Yes, where and when?**

Ping!

Almost instantly, as if waiting for my surrender. And there I went, pulled back into the whirlpool of choices and chances, desperately clinging to the flimsy life raft that was my remaining sense of self.

As I left the bathroom, the words **Rest in Piss** seemed to taunt me one last time, a call to rise from the filth and chaos that had ensnared me.

I pushed through the maze of the bathhouse, my path lit by the harsh blue light that had seeped into my soul. For better or worse, I was still here, still breathing, still clinging to whatever was left of me.

And so, I went to meet my client, my heart pounding in my chest, each step both an acceptance and a defiance of the shit show that was my life.

Walking down the alley, out of the bathhouse, the rain was relentless, pouring down in torrents as though the sky itself had unraveled. The yellow poncho I was wearing—Quinn's poncho—stuck to me like a second skin. The alley was dark, lit only by a single lamp post that gave off a dismal glow. The world was muted, as if covered by a shroud.

The night had been long, barely fruitful, and it was time for some rest. Just when I thought I'd finally get some peace—

My phone buzzed in my pocket, vibrating against my thigh. The screen flashed:

INCOMING CALL FROM THE DEVIL

Ignoring it, I continued walking, my heels clicking against the wet asphalt.

Ping!

PrideMate. Another reason to roll my eyes. What was it about desperation that made it so visible, so palpable to everyone but yourself?

Again, the screen lit up:

INCOMING CALL FROM THE DEVIL

Ping!
Buzz. Buzz.
Ping. Ping. Ping!

"FUCK OFF! AAAAHHH!" I screamed into the night, at the screen, at myself. I switched my phone off.

Just then, a voice sliced through the rain-soaked silence. "Ignoring me, Sexy?"

I turned to see a man—stranger, scruffy, eyes slightly off-kilter—approaching me with unsettling familiarity. His grin was all teeth, predator to prey.

"Saw you on PrideMate," he continued, sizing me up. "Vixen for cash or somethin', right?"

"I'm not in the mood," I retorted, feeling the weight of the night, of my life, pushing down on me.

"You a hooker?" he persisted, reaching for his wallet. "I've got cash, you know—what'll it be? Like fifteen or twenty or somethin'?"

I sighed, exasperated. "That's not what I do."

"What's wrong, dude?" he spat, lunging at me. "I'm fucking paying you."

His hand tightened around my neck, ripping the poncho as he pulled me closer. Panic surged through me. "GET OFF ME!" I screamed, pushing him away with all the force I could muster.

His eyes narrowed, his face contorted in ugly rage. "I'm not good enough for ya?" he snarled, grabbing my waist. "Is that it? HUH?! I'm not good enough for the PROSTITUTE?"

"Leave me the FUCK alone," I yelled, pushing him off me. I tried to throw a punch, but I was off-balance, shaky, missing my mark entirely.

WHAM!

His fist connected with my face, sending me sprawling onto the wet ground. My tarot cards flew out of my pocket, scattering in the puddles around me.

WHAM!

Another punch. Blood spurted from my mouth, mixing with the rain as it washed down the drain.

"Fucking whore," he spat, his words dripping with venom. He turned and ran, disappearing into the night.

I laid there, bruised and broken, clutching my torn yellow poncho. Around me, my tarot cards lay scattered and soiled, as if sharing in my degradation.

For a moment, I was alone—truly alone. The rain, indifferent to my plight, continued to fall, as if to cleanse or perhaps drown me. Lying on the cold, wet ground, every drop of rain felt like a searing needle, compounding the pain.

Among the strewn cards, **The Fool** stared back, its vibrant imagery a stark contrast to the surrounding gloom. Instead of promising new beginnings, it seemed to mock my misfortune.

The weight of the night, of all my choices, pressed down on me. The will to rise, to move, felt distant, almost nonexistent. With the rain streaming down, washing away tears and blood alike, I remained there, defeated, letting the storm consume the remnants.

♡ HELLO, DOLLY. ♡

"You're still goin' strong"

I stepped into my loft, soaked to the bone but grateful for the solitude.

What a fucking night.

Even amidst it all, my loft remained untarnished by my downward spiral. Near the corner, a vintage turntable delicately perched atop a worn-out suitcase, set on a rustic wooden crate. The sepia-toned memories associated with each vinyl that lay organized around the crate were both a salve and a thorn—comforting and painful in their contrasts to my current life. Adjacent to this makeshift music shrine stood a large, ornate mirror, doubling as a vanity. Countless times, it had reflected back my different avatars—some triumphant, some tragic. But tonight, it showcased one of horror.

My eye was swollen, my body a patchwork of aches and bruises, but in that moment, all I wanted was to feel something different. Anything different.

Taking in a deep breath, I approached the turntable, feeling the familiarity of the vinyl's textured grooves under my fingertips. A choice; an attempt to anchor myself amidst the storm of emotions. I set the needle down on "Hello, Dolly." As the rich notes and Dolly's unmistakable voice enveloped the room, memories of better times cascaded through my mind—a mingling of nostalgia and melancholy.

The song's cheerful greeting, likely to a familiar face, played through the speakers.

Ping!

A PrideMate notification. I smirked halfheartedly and twirled towards my vanity, ignoring it, as the song talked about greeting fellas.

Ping!

I sighed and sat down at the vanity, hesitating for a split second before daring to confront the reflection staring back at me. My eyes met my own in the mirror—bloodshot, but alive. My lips, once always carefully lined and glossed, were now cracked, with a streak of dried blood running down the corner.

I reached for my favourite shade of lipstick and carefully applied it, as if it were armour.

Dolly's voice conveyed a deep sentiment about returning home and feeling a sense of belonging.

I took off my shirt, revealing the constellation of bruises that decorated my torso. I winced, but my eyes never left the mirror.

Ping! Ping!

The phone buzzed again, but I ignored it, twirling my way to the bar.

Ping! Ping! Ping!

I rolled my eyes so hard I thought they'd get stuck. Tossing the phone onto the couch, I focused on making myself a cocktail. The ice clinked against the glass as if punctuating my thoughts. Cocktail in hand, I moved towards my pole, as if drawn by some magnetic force. Perhaps it was Dolly's voice swelling, depicting a room full of energy, spinning, and dance.

I grasped the pole and twirled around it, letting go for just a moment, feeling the world blur and my cocktail spill. But in that split second, I felt weightless, free.

The verse concluded with a promise of everlasting presence. Never leaving. Ever again.

Ping!

I downed my cocktail, grimacing as the liquid burned its way down my throat. For a brief, maddening moment, the room felt too small, too constricting.

With a guttural scream, I hurled my glass across the room.

CRASH!

The shards scattered across the floor, reflecting slivers of moonlight. My breaths were shallow, my body quivering. And I laughed. A laugh so maniacal, it reverberated through my soul, as tears dripped down my cheeks.

But I just stood there, amidst the fragments of a life I was still piecing together.

The chorus of men brought forth feelings of grandeur, of stage performances, and of recognition after a long absence.

As shards of glass sparkled like fallen stars, I slid down the pole, letting my emotions pour out. The lyrics were a siren call, reminding me of times when life felt grand, when every day was a performance and the world was my stage. But they also sang of homecomings and belonging, of recognizing oneself after a long absence. Sobs racked my body, a deluge escaping after being dammed up for too long.

Dolly's voice continued, its sentiment appreciating the beauty of someone, hinting at the admiration they still command.

I stroked the cold metal pole as if it were a comfort object, a grounding point in my free fall. Forcing a smile through the tears, I looked around the room.

My eyes settled on the nipple cover on the window, a relic from another life or perhaps another night.

The familiar refrain repeated, celebrating the subject's captivating allure.

Ping!

The promise of eternal presence echoed once more.

I spun around the pole, my eyes locking angrily onto the nipple cover, resentment surging through me.

And around.

Ping!

The refrain repeated, each repetition more insistent. And around again.

Ping. Ping. Ping!

The world spun faster, the room blurred, my emotions roiled—until—

CRASH!

The pole unscrewed from its base, sending me tumbling through the air. My temple smacked against the glass table with a sickening thud. Water from a toppled vase mixed with blood and smeared makeup. Everything was spinning, but my eyes focused on the static ceiling.

Sobbing heavily, my lips moved almost of their own accord. "Fuck," I mouthed, defeated and broken.

Tears streamed down my face, stinging the cuts and mixing with the crimson that stained the water on the floor. I laid there, gasping, each breath a challenge and a declaration all at once. And sometimes, that was enough. Sometimes, it had to be.

Sometimes we break things, not because we want to destroy them, but because we need to see them rearranged.

Through the haze, my eyes were drawn to a reddish glow that steadily pulsed through the night.

There it was, that damned heart-shaped neon sign outside my window. The glow was often a comfort on lonely nights, reminding me that life had its own rhythm. But tonight, it seemed to mock me.

Buzzing softly, almost in rhythm with my own racing heart, the neon light spelled out a word: **LOVE**. It was an ironic reminder of everything that seemed absent in my life right now. Its incessant glow was like a jab, poking at the gaping hole where love and self-worth should have resided.

"Love?" I spat bitterly, my voice breaking the heavy silence. "Is that what this is?!" I gestured wildly to the chaos around me. The state of my loft, my face, my life—

all in disarray, and that sign had the audacity to shine brightly, flaunting its message of love?

I wanted to scream at it, to shatter its neon tubes and plunge my world into darkness. I wanted it to know the pain and disillusionment that throbbed within me. I wanted to rip love out of the air, crumple it up, and throw it away. My fingers curled into tight fists, nails digging into my palms.

For a moment, I simply stood there, letting the anger wash over me. That stupid sign, with its simple message, felt like a cruel joke tonight. But as its glow continued to paint the room, it also cast light on my shattered reflection in the glass.

It was just a beacon, a reminder of something pure and good in the world, even if it felt out of reach for me in that moment. My anger slowly shifted, no longer directed at the outside world but inward, at the choices and circumstances that led me to this point.

Ping!

The phone pinged again, forgotten on the couch. But for the first time that night, I didn't care who or what was trying to reach me. I was busy, you see, with the delicate art of falling apart.

♡ DEER HUNT. ♡

"Bambi? You in here?"

Quiet. Dimly lit. Bambi's apartment's corridor always had the same eerie energy to it. Its gloom swallowed me whole, dripping with the kind of macabre energy that'd make even Hitchcock uneasy.

Amid the ambiance of the corridor, a torrent of emotions churned within me. The weight of untold secrets bore heavily on my conscience. I needed help, not just for the mess unfolding around me, but for the whirlwind of deceit and shadows I had created. Bambi deserved the truth, all of it.

It wasn't just about seeking help; it was about unburdening the soul, clearing the murky waters of deception. I needed to bare my soul to him. Tonight, I resolved to come clean about everything.

Each step, a limping waltz of pain and regret, guided me closer to Bambi's door. On the way, I glanced at the unit next door. Quinn's. It seemed to sneer at me from the periphery.

Nope.

Instead, I knocked delicately on Bambi's door. Too gentle. Too hesitant. Maybe I was hoping no one would hear it. Tired and weary, I leaned into the doorframe, and Quinn's door loomed large in my vision.

Not a sound.

I sighed and fished a key from its clandestine hiding spot—an air vent—and inserted it, the trembling of my hand echoing my internal disarray, into the lock. Twisting it until I heard the satisfying click. I pushed the door open, stepping into the dimness of Bambi's apartment. A knot formed in my stomach, a mix of dread and twisted relief.

"Bambi? You here?" My voice sliced through the heavy air, but there was no answer. Despite the urge to flee, I reached for the light switch. The sudden illumination revealed a living room untouched by chaos or struggle. Everything was in its place. Almost too much in its place.

I moved further into the apartment, navigating a path I'd walked many times before. But tonight, it felt like a maze. My breaths came out shallow, my body tensed as though expecting some hidden menace to leap out at me from the shadows. "Bambi? I-I need help—"

Then I rounded the corner. My eyes fell on Bambi's form crumpled on the floor, and my heart plummeted.

"BAMBI!"

I rushed to his side and checked for a pulse. It was there—thank God—but weak. Bambi looked like he'd been through hell. His face was a patchwork of bruises, a nasty gash sat above his eyebrow, and his arm lay twisted in an unnatural position. He was alive—barely. Every bruise, every cut, screamed of an untold horror.

My hands were shaking as I reached for my phone. I dialed 911, but hesitated before pressing 'call.' Could I really involve the authorities? Could I afford that exposure? Looking down at Bambi, I knew I had no choice.

I connected with emergency services. "My friend—my friend needs help. He's unconscious, and he looks really bad. I don't know what happened."

Minutes later, paramedics arrived, moving with a purpose and speed I seemed to lack these days. As they lifted Bambi onto a stretcher, one of them asked if I'd be accompanying them to the hospital.

I hesitated, then nodded. "Yeah, I'll follow. Just—just make sure he's okay."

They rushed out of the apartment, leaving me alone in the chaos of my own making. My thoughts raced but got nowhere. I wanted to escape, to disappear, to pretend none of this was happening. But for the first time in a long while, I knew I couldn't.

No more running.

I locked up Bambi's place and trudged back down the echoing corridor. My chest felt hollow, my limbs like lead, but for the first time in what felt like forever, I took a step. A step toward owning up to the mess that was my life, toward asking for the help I so desperately needed but had been too proud—or perhaps too scared—to seek.

The road to redemption was long and uncertain, but it was a journey I then realized I had to embark on.

For Bambi. For Quinn—

For myself.

♡ DEATH CARD. ♡

"Joshua. Scorpio. Montreal raised"

The walls of the hospital looked like they were last painted in the '60s, a moss green that might've been… "fashionable" back then but just looked depressing. The sheets were the kind of rough that made you miss your own bed. And the flickering fluorescents? I would have rather died. The kind of place that desperately needed Queer Eye.

Bambi was out cold in the bed beside me. Bandages around his head, hooked up to an IV, and God knew what else. He looked fragile and lost amidst the tangle of medical tubes.

The nurse, somewhere in her fifties, had finished up checking Bambi's vital signs. "I'll be down the hall," she said, as she left me alone with my thoughts.

I stared at Bambi, the harsh hospital lights painting him pallid, as a memory resurfaced—one that always brought a smirk to my face no matter the situation. The night we met.

It was one of those dodgy escorting gigs—the kind where you had to swig down a few shots just to muster the courage to walk through the door. I was the new kid on the block, lost in a sea of smoky eyes, seductive glances, and ostentatious personalities. Everywhere I turned, there was a poised, confident pro, and then there was Bambi.

Halfway through the evening, amidst an exceptionally dull conversation with a client, I'd spotted Bambi across the bar. With his ill-fitted wig that seemed to have a mind of its own and heels that were two sizes too big, he was trying to balance a tray of canapés. Just as our eyes met, Bambi's heels betrayed him, sending him crashing to the ground, but not before he flung the entire tray of canapés into a very expensive-looking fish tank.

The room had erupted in gasps and murmurs, but amidst the chaos, Bambi didn't care. Instead of embarrassment, he lay sprawled out, made a mock mermaid pose, and winked at me. It was ridiculous. It was hilarious. It was a bold middle finger to the elitist events we would then partake in for the years to come.

I remember laughing out loud, the first genuine laugh of the evening. Bambi had instantly felt like a soulmate—not fitting in, but with an undeniable authenticity. By the end of that night, we were inseparable, two outcasts against the world, and the beginning of many unpredictable adventures together. And now here he was, another victim to my chaos. A chaos that pulled in everyone who ventured too close. Angel, Kitty, Aspen—

Quinn…

I remembered the first night I'd spent with Quinn. The room was filled with the musky scent of gin, the rustling of bedsheets, and the obscure allure of tarot cards. With a couple ominous pulls—

And then it hit me. **Death**.

The second draw of the night. A card so ominously unclear. I always hated when it showed up.

I chuckled bitterly. Transformation. Right. The past few days replayed in my mind's eye like a twisted highlight reel… a perfect symbol of my unraveling, of dancing on the edge and courting disaster with a forced smile. It was this continuous dance with disaster, every step choreographed by my own reckless choices. Always self-destructive. Gigs gone wrong. The relentless act of playing the misunderstood loner. Jay…

But as I sat there, in that poorly lit, cold hospital room, a profound epiphany took root. Maybe **Death** wasn't a prediction but a prescription. Maybe it was time to—change.

I considered the possibility of rebirth. Could I, like a phoenix, rise from the ashes? Could there be a version of me that was deserving of love? But then it hit me—

'Love'. Why was I obsessed with love?

Selling it. Craving it. Always looking for it at the wrong places... and never finding it.

All while presenting a facade—a caricature of who I truly was. Keeping everyone at an arm's length, never letting anyone peer into the depths that Quinn always alluded to—as he would put it, the 'real' me.

The real me. Huh.

Death. The dawn of a new beginning.

One that had remained elusive, seeming almost alien. What about the idea of some type of love that had been overlooked, dismissed as improbable for someone like me. A love of—

Self.

And in that moment, propelled by that four letter word, I knew exactly what I had to do.

My fingers hovered over my phone, hesitating for just a second before I dialled a number. He picked up almost immediately.

"Thought about my offer," Jay's voice filtered through the speaker.

"I'm leaving," I said. My voice was flat, devoid of the emotion I was swallowing down. "Maybe out of town, out of the country. Who knows... the police will be here soon to get Bambi's statement. They'll track you down eventually. So don't bother doing anything stupid."

My fingers tapped on the edge of the chair, and I could feel my teeth grinding together.

Love.

"You know," I began, my voice tinged with bitterness, "feelings are a pretty fucked up concept. I used to think nobody would ever love me, except maybe you. But what you did—what you've been doing—it's not love. Never was. You just took advantage of a lonely boy... and broke him."

I thought back to when I first met Jay. The charm, the promises, the way he made me feel like I was on top of the world. It was intoxicating. But as time wore on, the mask began to slip, revealing the puppeteer behind the scenes, always pulling strings, always orchestrating. The emotional manipulation, the gaslighting, the subtle ways he would erode my confidence just to build it back up, making me entirely dependent on his approval.

It was never about the money, not really. It was about power. Jay thrived on it, the way he could bend people to his will, manipulate situations to his advantage. I'd been caught in his web, and every attempt to break free only seemed to tighten the noose.

I remembered the nights when I'd lie awake, tormented by the power he held over me, feeling trapped, like a bird in a cage. And as much as I wanted to hate him, a part of me was addicted—the danger, the high stakes. It was a twisted game, one where I constantly felt like a pawn, yet inexplicably kept coming back for more.

Love.

The cruel reality was that Jay didn't just want to own my debts; he wanted to own my soul. To have me at his beck and call, ready to jump through hoops, forever dancing to his tune. And the scariest part? At times, he almost succeeded. But as I stared into the cold, calculating eyes of **The Devil** on my phone screen, a flicker of defiance rose within me. I was not his to own. Not anymore.

"You've got your money. Bambi and Quinn will get their lives back, and you'll never see me—ever again."

Self.

I hung up and stared at my phone for a second. Then I blocked his contact. "Bye, Jay," I whispered, more to myself than to him.

Reaching into my bag, I pulled out Bambi's pink cat ear headphones and started to scribble on a small piece of paper. I knew what I had to do. It was always obvious.

I set them gently on the table next to him. It was a promise, to Bambi and to myself.

As I sat there, I realized something had shifted inside me. A line had been drawn, a cycle finally broken. Even in that decrepit room, I felt the stirrings of a future, one that for the first time in a long while, seemed like it might be my own.

I could finally breathe. When—

The door creaked open behind me, a draft of cold air momentarily displacing the stuffy hospital atmosphere. "I got your message," Quinn murmured softly, each syllable laced with a mix of concern and anticipation.

My heart sank, suddenly burdened by the weight of what I had just written to Bambi, and now had to tell Quinn. Wiping away a tear that had escaped its duct, I turned to face him.

"How's he doing?" His voice was tinged with palpable concern, eyes so blue they could have been stolen from the ocean itself.

"He'll be fine," I whispered, each word a promise I prayed I could keep—not just for Bambi but for myself.

"And… are you okay?" Quinn's question hung in the air, delicate and vulnerable, like a leaf on the edge of falling.

Here we go. No more mask.

A smile broke across my face, fragile but real. This was my moment to reciprocate the vulnerability he had offered me weeks ago, an unspoken dialogue about personal things—

"Joshua. Scorpio. Montreal raised," I began, each word a stone paving a new path between us. "I'm surprisingly good at Rock, Paper, Scissors, just like you. I believe red to be the superior colour."

A light sparked in Quinn's eyes, a recognition that I was finally letting him in. We shared a momentary laugh, a cathartic release that danced around the room.

"I hate asparagus. Long story…" I continued, chuckling at the incongruity of that story. "Probably for another time. I had a really weird obsession with foxes for a while. They're just so cute—explains the name I guess." Our laughter melded together, sweet and cleansing, like a long-awaited rain.

Taking a deep breath, I ventured into murkier waters. "I ran away at eighteen. With a guy—Jay… who promised me the world, but ended up shattering it." Our eyes met, and I saw no pity, only understanding. "You know, it's funny. You think everything's shitty at home until you actually leave. I was too ashamed to go back, so I did what I do best. I just kept running… and running."

My heart pounded in my chest, as I continued, each word tinged with a vulnerability I had never allowed myself before. "And um… I was abused, by someone who should have been a friend. And Jay saved me—well, um… he killed him actually—choked him to death right in front of me. Which I guess is why—"

"Don't touch the neck," Quinn whispered, completing my sentence. His eyes were watery, but the smile on his face was pure tenderness.

I chuckled, a short, shaky sound. "Yeah, don't touch the neck. Anyways…"

Quinn's voice grew softer, full of gentle regret. "I'm sorry, Vixen… I definitely deserved that slap on the dance floor."

I laughed again, this time more freely. "You know, for a long time, I thought Jay was my hero. But how could I? Heroes don't wear mustard-stained tank tops—"

"I'm starting to think they wear cowboy hats," I mused, locking eyes with Quinn. There was clarity in that moment—a radiant, poignant clarity that pushed away the darkness that had so long hovered over me.

Quinn glanced at the pink cat-ear headphones and the note next to Bambi's bedside. "You're leaving."

It wasn't a question; it was an acknowledgment—a consent of sorts, as if he understood that I had to tear myself away to heal. To grow. To be better.

"The Death card," he spoke softly, eyes meeting mine.

I exhaled, my breath shaky. "The Death card—the end of one chapter, the beginning of another. I need to… get away from it all, for a while. And who knows, I might come back a different person."

Quinn chuckled, though his eyes were moist. "Oh GOD! Not a different person?! Are you telling me that I'm gonna have to start ALL OVER—with THAT one?! Jesus,

Vixen. You really like to make a guy work for it, don't you!"

In that instant, as we smiled through unshed tears and bittersweet emotions, I knew it had to be done. "It's better that way. For everyone," I emphasized, allowing the gravity of the moment to sink in. "Lie low please? I've been involved with some pretty violent dicks."

Quinn smiled. "Don't worry about me. I'm not going anywhere… besides—" he assured me, his eyes steady, a lighthouse guiding me through stormy seas, "You'll need someone here, when you come back."

As we locked eyes, it felt like the universe paused, wrapping us in a cocoon of timelessness, our collective pain and hope, regrets and wishes, coalescing into one ineffable moment.

"Walk me home?" he asked, his voice imbued with a hope that was both heartbreaking and beautiful.

And as we shared that heavy, lingering gaze, I felt the dawn of something new; terrifying yet incredible, like the first rays of light breaking the horizon after the longest night of my life.

The dawn was breaking, a soft pastel palette of colours washing over the sky as if an artist had decided to paint a new beginning for me. It was 5:15 AM, a time when the world was at its quietest, almost holding its breath in reverence to the serenity of the hour.

The alley was bathed in that early morning light, each puddle reflecting a fragmented sky, like pieces of a puzzle yearning for completion. Birds broke the silence, their chirps a distant background score that somehow underscored the gravity of the moment. They were free, unfettered by past or future, and I envied them for it.

Quinn and I walked on opposite ends of the alley, a physical space between us that felt at once too short and too long. An invisible pull seemed to link us, a delicate balance of wanting and uncertainty, fear and longing. It was as if the universe had choreographed this moment, a dance where each step was fraught with meaning but executed in silence.

Our eyes met intermittently, making contact for a fleeting second before darting away. Each glance felt like a conversation, questions and answers exchanged without uttering a word. "Are you sure about this?" His eyes seemed to ask. "I have to be," mine replied.

It's fascinating how silence can be so loud, how it can say things that words often fail to capture.

As we approached the end of the alley, I knew that another threshold was upon me. This was more than just concrete meeting cobblestone; it was the juncture of endings and beginnings, goodbyes and hellos, fears and hopes.

Our footsteps became slower, reluctantly drawing out the seconds. We both knew that at the end of this alley was an unwritten page, an open field of possibilities that could only be explored by stepping into the unknown.

And as we finally reached that boundary, our eyes locked one last time. A whole universe of emotions swirled in that gaze, love and regret, apprehension and understanding, all mingling to form a complex tapestry that only we could comprehend.

The birds' chirping crescendoed as if in acknowledgment of our bittersweet parting, their song a farewell anthem that carried with it the weight of our unspoken words.

And then we stepped out of the alley, each turning in opposite directions. But as I walked away, I felt a strange sensation, a warmth in the pit of my stomach that reassured me in spite of everything.

Because I knew that whatever lay ahead, we had already transcended the sum of our pasts, the weight of our mistakes, the burden of our fears. We were more than the space between us; we were the words unspoken, the feelings unfelt, the life unlived.

We were the silence, and the silence was beautiful—

Just when he asked me, "wanna come in?"

♡ DANCE WITH ME. ♡

"So this is how it all ends"

The atmosphere inside Quinn's apartment was like a fragile truce. The curtains billowed softly as if sighing, catching a light breeze that had wandered in through the open window. It felt like a sanctuary from the world outside, a tiny pocket of tranquility where the outside world's clamour could be kept at bay, if only for a few moments.

Quinn headed for the couch, pausing to look back at me as I stood by the door, my hand still resting on the frame.

"You can come in if you want," he asked, breaking the delicate silence that had settled between us.

I nodded, a simple gesture that carried a myriad of unspoken feelings: regret, longing, a sense of an ending.

My heart was a heavy pendulum swinging between two extremes—wanting to stay and needing to leave.

"So this is how it all ends, huh?" Quinn said, sinking into the couch. He smiled at me, a poignant blend of melancholy and affection, as if he were trying to memorize every detail of my face.

"I was expecting something grander from—the great Dolly himself," he quipped.

I returned his smile, though mine was tinged with sadness. It was an uneasy grin, born out of knowing what we were both thinking but were afraid to articulate. "Life rarely gives us the endings we expect," my smile said.

Quinn's eyes twinkled with an invitation. "Dance with me."

My heart clenched. A dance felt both like an end and a beginning, a full circle moment that seemed almost too perfect for the situation we found ourselves in. I walked over, pulled him up from the couch, and pressed myself against him, arms wrapping around his body as if trying to capture the essence of the moment.

"Thank you, Quinn," I said, tears blurring my vision. The simple phrase was a summation of all the words I couldn't say, a summation of my gratitude for his presence in my life, no matter how brief or complicated.

"For what?" Quinn asked, but his eyes already knew. They always did.

"Everything," I whispered, trembling as if I were a fragile thing about to break.

We swayed together, our bodies finding a natural rhythm that spoke of intimacy and knowing, each movement a paragraph in a story that was coming to an end. Quinn's face brushed against my hair, and I felt him breathe me in, as if he too were committing this moment to memory.

"I'm so sorry," I finally uttered, the words catching in my throat.

We didn't need to elaborate. "Sorry" was a stand-in for all the regrets, the missed opportunities, the what-ifs that would linger in the air long after I'd walked out the door.

And as we danced, I felt a bittersweet symphony of emotions rise within me—regret and relief, sorrow and a glimmer of hope—all swirled together in that single, fragile moment of human connection.

That's what this was, after all, a human moment. A moment of understanding, of farewell, of love in its most complex form. A moment that neither of us would ever forget, no matter where our separate paths would lead us.

Because Quinn was love—once-felt, forever etched; a beacon in the ephemeral dance of hearts.

Time stopped.

For a second, suspended in time, it felt as if the world had faded away. It was just Quinn and I, swaying in an empty room where love seemed a very simple, very possible thing. Quinn's eyes were like an endless ocean, and I was ready to dive in, ready to finally say it—

"I do love you, Qui—"

BANG!

And reality shattered.

The words were stolen by a roar that filled the room, dissonant and final. The chorus of our shared heartbeat interrupted. My eyes widened in disbelief, locking onto a cruel scarlet bloomed against the pristine white of Quinn's shirt, spreading like wildfire, consuming all that stood in its path.

BANG! BANG!

Quinn's body fell to the ground, his eyes that once held galaxies now clouded with pain and confusion, gravity pulling him away as if the world itself couldn't bear our happiness.

"I fucking told you—"

The voice was a jagged knife, twisted and malevolent, venomous and dripping with malice. My body turned, my heart pounding in my chest as if trying to escape the cage of my body, but my soul already knew who stood there.

It was Jay.

Smoke was still curling from his gun, his eyes burning holes into my soul. Beside him—

Angel stared in sheer horror, her eyes dilating in real-time disbelief.

"You—you said we'd just scare him—" Her voice was tinged with regret, a weak attempt to retreat from the hellish scene unfolding.

"You selfish FUCK, Vixen," Jay spat, stepping closer, gun still aimed at me.

"Quinn," I choked, my voice barely rising above a whisper. "Quinn?"

The silence was louder than any reply. Quinn lay unmoving. Unresponsive.

"You're mine," Jay hissed, seizing my throat as if he could force his twisted form of love into me.

"When will that get into that dumb little head of yours, DOLL."

Something broke within me—years of bottled fury, indignation, abuse—all erupting in a primal scream of resistance. "I'M NOT. A FUCKING. DOLL!"

My knuckles cracked. A neon bulb screeched. In a moment that seemed to unfold in slow motion, yet happened faster than a heartbeat, I broke free from Jay's grasp. When—

WHAM!

Jay's blood splashed onto my face like cruel paint on an unfinished canvas. Hot and viscous.

Eyes gaping. Time frozen. There it was—a knife. Jutting out of Jay's throat like a terrible answer to an unasked question. A final, strangled gurgle escaped his lips, with his final gaze locked onto me, forever unyielding, even in death.

As he collapsed to the floor, Angel appeared behind him, her face a tableau of shock, guilt, and regret—her eyes vacantly wide, her chest heaving in post-adrenal shock.

"I'm—"

Angel's voice shivered, her lips trembling as if the very words were shards of glass.

I wiped Jay's blood from my lips. My eyes—once a sanctuary for suppressed emotion—were now cold, impenetrable fortresses.

"I can't..." Angel gasped.

My eyes locked onto hers. In that brief exchange, a lifetime of choices, regrets, and consequences seemed to weigh down on us both. Angel had made her choice, and so had I. The repercussions would chase us, haunt us for the rest of our lives, but in that moment, there was only silence—a deafening, overwhelming silence that drowned out even the loudest of screams.

And yet, in this unspeakable silence, a million words were conveyed in a single, fractured moment. I felt as if I were suffocating under the weight of choices made, lives destroyed, and a future that had slipped through my fingers like grains of sand.

What remained were broken pieces of a life I had to somehow piece back together. But not here. Not now. For now, there was only a gaping emptiness, a sorrow so profound that it hollowed me out, leaving nothing but the shell of a man who had loved, and lost, more deeply than I had ever thought possible.

The whirling blue and red police lights splashed through the curtains, creating a surreal dance of shadows on the walls. I could hear footsteps hammering up the stairs, echoing like a drumbeat in my head, counting down to something horrific—something final. I already knew what that was.

My knees buckled, and I stumbled back to Quinn's lifeless form. Reality seemed suspended, paused for this fragile, desperate moment.

"Quinn… come on Quinn," I choked out, my voice scarcely more than a whisper, broken by sobs that I couldn't suppress. It was as if I was trying to breathe life back into him through my words, knowing all too well the futility of it. "Quinn?… please."

"Check that unit," a stern muffled voice coming from down the corridor.

"Vixen… let's go—" Angel implored. Reaching my ears, but it was like she was calling me from another world, another lifetime.

I can't leave him. Not like this.

Ignoring her, I wrapped myself around Quinn. I clenched my hands into fists, my nails digging into the fabric of his shirt, as if I could anchor him back to life.

No. No, no, no.

Trembling, I lifted him just off the ground, swaying side to side. And with all the pain in the world, I whispered—

"Dance with me."

It was a dance; a dance of sorrow, a dance of finality.

"No one's there. I'll try this one," a muffled voice sounded closer now.

WHAM! WHAM!

The door echoed under the pounding.

"Police—open up!"

Angel sprinted to me, panic lighting her eyes, her voice tinged with a hysteria that mirrored my own. "Vixen. We need to go. NOW."

I pressed my lips against Quinn's cold forehead. "I'm sorry," I whispered through a torrent of ugly sobs. My entire being was consumed with the visceral, gnawing pain of finality.

WHAM! WHAM! WHAM!

The pounding on the door grew louder, more urgent. The door screamed in agony as it splintered. Angel grabbed my arm, pulling me away from Quinn, dragging me towards the window.

But I had to look back. Just once more. I needed to remember him. Scar him in. Brand him to my soul.

My eyes met Quinn's, or rather the place where the spark that had once been Quinn resided. It was an abyss, and I felt my entire being swallowed whole.

BAM!

The door exploded inward just as Angel yanked me to my feet, as we lunged onto the cold, wet metal of the fire escape.

The air sliced through me as I jumped down, each blow rung a descent into a future without Quinn. I had no plan, no direction, no purpose other than the primitive urge to escape, to survive. My body moved of its own accord, every muscle, every sinew committed to the primal, senseless act of running. But no matter how fast my legs carried me, I knew I was sprinting on the edge of an abyss, a chasm opened by Quinn's death, which would haunt me until the end of my days.

And somewhere, in the shattered remains of that moment, I thought of Quinn—his smile, his cerulean blues, his voice. He was right after all...

A part of me would forever dance with him, in a place untouched by time, violence, or the haunting flicker of neon memories. But for now, there was only this—this broken, bloody now—and empty vessels.

♡ ARCHANGEL. ♡

"Hey Jackass! I'm still waiting on that fifty dollars"

Fucking sunlight.

The rays felt like a blade cutting through my raw skin, each beam striking me as if saying, "Life goes on." I limped through the alley, my makeup smeared from tears I no longer had the strength to shed. All around me, the mistresses of the night stumbled home, high heels in hand, their faces a testament to decisions they'd probably regret later. I remembered that time, where I too stood among them. Smiling. Cocky as hell. They were women of the evening; I was a man of the moment—a moment that had shattered me.

"Vixen, I—"

Angel's voice was laced with regret, each word a pitiful attempt to sew up the gash that had been torn open in my soul. I couldn't even bring myself to look at her. My gaze was focused on some undefined point in the distance, a point I wasn't even sure existed.

"I didn't think he'd—" Her voice trembled, failing her as she swallowed the rest of the sentence. "Vixen, can you slow down?"

"I have to get home," I replied, my voice as flat as the pavement under my feet.

"I'm not leaving you."

"I'm fine."

"Vixen—"

I wheeled around, my eyes locking onto hers, fierce but dry. No more tears. "Comes with the gig, you know that."

For a moment, her eyes widened, absorbing the full weight of my words—each syllable like a drop of acid, corrosive and raw. I was trying to keep it together, trying to withhold the deluge that was always one blink away.

"He was just a client," I said, my voice barely more than a whisper now. "And… it wasn't your fault, Angel."

I sniffled, a pathetic sound that said more than any words could. "You—you karmic Angel."

Turning away from her shocked expression, I continued on my path, leaving Angel rooted to the spot. When a ghost from my past shouted amidst the hurls of her night—

"Hey Jackass! I'm still waiting on that fifty dollars," Roxy called out from a corner.

The cosmic joke. The satire. And me, the eternal fool.

Normally, I'd have a witty comeback, but now, nothing. I continued to move, feet barely touching the ground, lost in the labyrinth of my own thoughts, each one a haunting echo of the life and love I'd just lost.

I was in a free fall, plunging into an abyss of despair and emptiness, each step taking me further away from the world I knew, and deeper into a crevasse of darkness that had opened up inside me.

And as I walked away, the distance between Angel and me seemed to widen with every step, a chasm not just of space but of understanding, of life experiences so dark, so painful, that they couldn't be bridged by comforting words or good intentions.

It didn't matter. Nothing mattered anymore. I was adrift in an endless sea of hurt, and all the ships had sailed, leaving me behind. And with that, I reached my loft.

I closed the door behind me, its gentle click echoing in the solitary confinement that was my loft. An unassuming sound that marked the end of one chapter and hesitated on the precipice of the next.

I glanced around my home. It was supposed to be a sanctuary, but now, every corner, every shadow seemed to mock me, filled with memories and moments that I would never relive. Inhaling sharply, I exhaled the breath I didn't know I was holding.

My reflection in the mirror was a cruel joke, a grotesque caricature of the person I used to be. But what caught my eye and stole my breath was the dark, reddish-brown stain on my white blouse—Quinn's blood. A haunting tattoo, a permanent reminder of what had been ripped from me.

I grabbed a sponge and started scrubbing furiously at the bloodstain, the water turning a murky pink as I did.

Come off.

My hands moved of their own accord, my arms fuelled by a desperation to erase, to cleanse, to forget.

Come off.

The tears began to flow then, hot and unchecked, streaming down my face as I scrubbed harder and harder.

Come back.

And then I stopped.
Frozen.
The stain wasn't going away. No matter how hard I scrubbed, it clung to the fabric, stubborn and unyielding. Quinn. When a sudden sound made me jump—

Ping!

The sound of my PrideMate notification broke the spell, shattering the silence like a rock through glass. I stood there, staring at the heart-shaped neon sign ahead of me, sniffing back the remnants of my tears.

No. No more.

The word '**LOVE**' flickered sporadically, as if even the sign itself was unsure of its meaning.

That sign... that fucking sign. I felt as if it was mocking me, dangling the one thing I had lost, the one thing that had been snatched away right before I could truly grasp it. I always hated that sign.

A beacon of my past, a symbol of the countless nights where I sold fleeting versions of love, transactional and hollow. A constant reminder that love, once commodified, lost its essence.

But was it really just the past? Or was it also the universe posing a question, challenging me at my most vulnerable? Was this a choice presented to me in cold, glowing neon: to go back to the easy, soulless sale of love or to embark on the arduous journey of seeking genuine self-love?

I gazed up at the sign, lost in its luminous glow. The oscillating light painted patterns on my face, casting shadows that danced in tandem with the riot of emotions surging within me. It was like a cruel, cosmic test, asking me if I would yield to the seductive allure of old habits or forge a new path forward.

That sign. That fucking sign.

An artifact from my past, a haunting prophecy, and a premonition—all wrapped into a single, glaring symbol.

It whispered of nights filled with artificial affection and the hollow echoes of laughter. It murmured tales of fleeting touches, transient connections, and empty promises.

And yet, it also beckoned, hinting at the possibility of redemption, of starting anew. To break away from the cycle, to reject the lure of old patterns and truly embrace a love that was genuine, nurturing, and self-affirming.

My fingers twitched, itching to open PrideMate, to drown the pain in the familiar yet empty embrace of the past. But something held me back—a newfound resolve, a glimmer of hope, or perhaps the lingering imprint of Quinn's love.

I took a deep breath, the cool night air filling my lungs, cleansing the suffocating weight of grief, if only for a fleeting moment. Taking one last look at the neon sign:

No more selling love.

It was time to discover its true essence, to nurture it, cherish it, and allow it to heal the gaping wounds within.

Mechanically, I reached for my suitcase, flipping off the light switch. I was done. Done with this place, this life, this skin that I couldn't crawl out of. Standing there for a moment in the dimness, about to step into a future unshackled by my past, my flaws, my toxic ways.

Ping!

Another PrideMate message. Reluctantly, my eyes flicked down to the screen.

(Regg): **Hey? You free tonight for a few hours? PNP.**

PNP. Party and Play. A euphemism for my drug-fuelled sexual encounters. An escape. Perhaps. Or my undoing.

My thumb hovered over the delete button. I paused, my hand gripping the handle of my suitcase, clutching my fur coat stained with Quinn's blood. I squeezed it tight, each fibre a thread of the past, of love, of agony.

The test.

Can I truly walk away?

In that pregnant pause, my eyes closed...
My entire life seemed to hang in the balance...
And then...
I failed.
My hand loosened its grip on the suitcase handle.
With a forced smile that masked a sea of inner turmoil, I dropped the suitcase. It landed with a dull thud, a sound

as final as a closing chapter, yet as haunting as an unfinished story.

I knew then, standing alone in my darkened loft, that I had chosen. I chose my vices over my salvation, my past over my future, my pain over the love I'd lost and the love I could've found.

And in that choice, I remained a prisoner, shackled not by fate, but by my own unwillingness to change, to grieve, to love.

Fuck it.

♡ THE TOWER. ♡

"Hello, Dolly. See you tonight"

The room was awash in the sinister glow of the heart-shaped neon sign, its red hue casting a spell that blurred the line between love and danger. Spreading its haze over shattered dreams and fractured promises. Each flicker of the sign seemed to echo the volatile unpredictability of my life—always on the verge of burning out, but clinging stubbornly to some fragile semblance of luminosity. A dying star.

I shuffled the tarot cards, an act devoid of spiritual significance now, their edges worn like old friends. My drink was more a chalice of sorrow than a cocktail, its bitterness a cruel reminder of the life I'd led.

Reggie, some PrideMate client with an obnoxiously large neck tattoo, sprawled on the couch, blissfully sinking into the chemical heaven he'd just inhaled. A temporary escape from a world neither of us fully understood. "I feel it kicking in, man. This is fucking amazing. You feel it?"

I ignored him, my gaze drifting instead to the nipple cover sealed to the window cracks—a crude, yet hauntingly poetic seal over wounds. As though holding together the shards of my shattered past. It was both a relic and a memento, sealing not just the window but a chapter of my life. Quinn's handwritten note on it whispered, **Hello, Dolly. See you tonight**. A sacrament of love and pain, as stuck in the in-between as I was.

My tarot cards were laid before me, the archaic figures barely visible under the room's demonic tint. I drew one—**The Tower.**

A symbol of upheaval, of chaos, of a foundation so shattered it can only bring about absolute rebirth or ruinous descent. A monolith of chaos and crumbling foundations, symbolic of catastrophic transformation. It was as if the card was Quinn, was Reggie, was me—all of us, volatile and crumbling, always falling but never landing. Laughable.

"When's your birth date?" I finally asked.

"June sixteen, nineteen ninety-five. Why?" Reggie mumbled, his eyes lazily tracing invisible patterns on the ceiling.

A shiver crawled up my spine; Quinn. "Gemini. With an... Aquarius moon."

A half-hearted laugh escaped me. I tossed the card onto the table and looked at Reggie. "Dance with me," I implored, setting aside all the cosmic warnings. The neon sign buzzed louder, as if jeering at my attempt to extract a moment's peace from the chaos.

He looked at me, puzzled and bemused, but I was unyielding. "Just... come." My words were a hymn, a summons.

I downed my drink in a single gulp and moved closer to him. "Dance."

As if in a trance, Reggie extended his hand, and the next moment we were entwined, slow dancing amidst a haze of cigarette smoke and unresolved tensions on the stripper pole's podium. High above the ground. In our own little castle.

I pressed my head against his chest, momentarily drowning in the rhythmic beating of his heart. Slow dancing, spinning, to the pace. I felt the quiet desperation of trying to connect to a heartbeat other than my own. It was as if, for those few seconds, I was desperately trying to steal a fragment of his vitality, his unwounded spirit. But all I could think, all I could imagine—

Was Quinn. There, in his place.

Reggie's fingers gently combed through my hair. I tightened my grip around him, my body trembling. A memory of what had been done to me time and time again by that cowboy.

That stupid lil' smirk.

But chaos, as represented by **The Tower**, always reigns. And suddenly…

Reggie backed onto my red rhinestone thong—
Loosing balance on one of its glimmering gems—
And tripped.
Sending us flying off the edge.

As we plummeted from the podium, we lurched dangerously towards the fractured window. My heart stopped. Just when—

As if guided by some twisted guardian angel, Reggie managed to grab hold of the stripper pole, pulling us back from the brink of disaster. Our eyes met, and the neon sign flickered and buzzed ominously above us, its luminescent heart reflecting in my eyes.

Time stood still as I teetered on the edge of that podium. Head hanging back, hand clasped to Reggie's tank top. I stared out the fractured window, at the neon heart that seemed to buzz in a manic crescendo—a harbinger of doom or salvation, I couldn't tell.

The heart, flashing incessantly, was like a beacon—summoning, challenging, mocking me. A reminder of my tumultuous relationship with love—both received and given. It was as if the neon sign was not just an adornment on a building outside, but a reflection of the insistent drumming of my own heart—a heart that, despite its many injuries, never stopped beating.

The buzzing grew louder, filling the room until it was the only sound. Reggie's grip on the stripper pole slackened, a frantic moment unfurled in slow motion. The universe paused, allowing me to soak in the heart-shaped irony above, its haunting reflection bouncing off my pupils.

Head hanging back, I turned my gaze from the neon sign to the ground below. How many times had I stared out that window, drawn by the call of the ground? The three stories felt much more like a tower in a dark fairy tale, with me as its tragic prisoner.

The height that once brought me vertigo was now a beckoning abyss. My life had always been a tightrope walk, teetering between self-acceptance and societal expectations, between love's tender embrace and its cruel chokehold.

The Tower's prophecy unfolded in neon letters: a simple proposition cloaked in insidious meaning. Yet in that moment of reckoning, it was as if the universe itself was granting me permission to collapse so I could finally rebuild. It was an invitation, a challenge, and a release all wrapped into one.

I breathed in, time elongating like taffy, savouring the momentary silence that followed. Hand gripped to Reggie's tank top. Holding on for dear life. When—

Ping!

That fucking ping. Always puppeteering me.

I looked up one last time at the neon sign, its red light gleaming like the devil's eye, and realized it had always been pointing toward this single, fateful moment. An epiphany as I balanced above the void. The neon sign— love twisted into a toxic parody—now seemed to hum in approval of my finite nature.

I smiled, my grip on Reggie's tank top loosening. I could easily pull myself back up, but—

For the first time in my life, the strings were cut, the marionette was free. And I finally chose—

I let go.

Falling off the podium, I stared back at Reggie. His eyes growing wide with shock. But I couldn't be bothered. This wasn't about him. This was for me. My courageous, eyes-wide-open plunge into the uncertainty that I had longed to face on my own terms. And—

CRASH!

I crashed through the fractured window, plummeting from the third floor in a surreal descent of glass shards, body glitter, and that lone, heart-shaped nipple cover. A descent both literal and metaphorical. But the height didn't bother me. Nor did the fall.

This constant battle with myself. This struggle to find self-love in a sea of impermanence. The shit show that was my core… all culminated to this final assertion of agency in a life that seemed hell-bent on denying me any control.

In that plummeting descent, there was empowerment—a final act of reclaiming control over my narrative, no longer at the mercy of anyone or anything. The very ground that I once gazed upon with trepidation was now my chosen destiny.

I finally get to choose.

The night air rushed against my face, every gust a caress, every droplet a baptism, as Quinn's note seemed to float beside me—a guardian angel of sharpie and fabric, forever tethered to both my past and my final act of liberation. In that descent, I tasted peace. My eyes never wavered from that nipple cover, the last physical thing anchoring me to a world I was leaving behind.

Hello, Dolly. See you tonight!

A cruel and intimate irony scrawled in ink, sealing my fate. But the tiny heart-shaped nipple cover wasn't just a piece of apparel; it was a keepsake of a love that was as fierce as it was destructive. Floating alongside me in my final act, the show, it had become the last tangible link to a past that I was shedding but could not fully escape. As much as it signified my relationship with Quinn, it also encapsulated my perpetual yearning for something, perhaps—real, something enduring in a world of fleeting distractions.

Kitty had her lollipop. Aspen his rings. Emma her cigarette. And Angel her bubble of gum—And this… this little nipple cover—It was my talisman. My curse. Sealed to the fractured window of my life as surely as my fate was sealed to the choices I made.

As gravity claimed me, I felt a wave of liberation, of resignation, of finality. I breathed in the night air one final time, as I descended toward the cold, wet concrete below.

Every fall, no matter how devastating, can be a leap of faith. A faith that, in some other realm or reality, the radiant warmth of unconditional self-love awaits, eclipsing every shadow, every hurt, every judgment. A place where the neon signs don't just buzz—they shine.

Resigned, relieved, almost peaceful—I breathed in one last gulp of the night air, eyes never wavering away from Quinn's note, and allowed myself a small, knowing—

Smirk.

No fear. No regret. Just acceptance of a life lived on the edge, within a world that was perpetually night.

My last thought before colliding with the unforgiving ground below wasn't of remorse or sorrow. It was a simple, solitary wish:

"Let the next world I fall into be filled with sunlight."

A promise that, wherever I am, my quest for light—true light, not the deceiving glow of a neon sign or the ephemeral flicker of a phone screen—continues.

May I fall into a world that, even if spent on the edge of the underworld, or amidst heartbreaking farewells and chaotic undoings, however flawed or broken, that always, always yearns for sunlight.

But for now,
For this strange little lifetime,
The darkness?
Well, Hun—

It always felt like home.

ABOUT THE AUTHOR.

Vixen's journey is as multifaceted as the Tarot cards he once read as an escort. Navigating the complex layers of human desire and connection, he found solace and understanding within them and his clients.

Born into a world of ephemeral connections and societal judgment, Vixen navigated a path riddled with challenges. Yet, amidst the chaos and the nights that seemed to stretch into oblivion, he discovered an inner strength, a voice that had been stifled for too long. His experiences, both tumultuous and tender, and his search for connection through his Tarot abilities, laid the foundation for his debut novel.

An author who intertwines shadow and light, Vixen channels his unique experiences into his writing, painting authentic tales of love, loss, and self-discovery. His prose resonating with vulnerability and fierce determination, painting a portrait of a soul in search of meaning.

"Rent Boy" delves deep into the complexities of love—not just romantic love, but self-love, and the courage it takes to reclaim one's power in a world that often seeks to diminish it.

It's about confronting the darkest corners of existence, challenging societal norms, and emerging with a love that is pure, unwavering, and transcendent. Through his words, he beckons readers to embark on a journey of introspection and, ultimately, liberation.

Beyond the written word, Vixen continues to push boundaries, using his artistic platform to destigmatize the lives of escorts, to challenge societal constructs, and to invite readers to delve into the depths of their own Shadows through Tarot.

He has passionately ventured into the world of tarot design, recently releasing two bespoke decks. Drawing from his own darkness, he's committed to assisting others in their personal journeys, helping them embrace and learn from the shadows within.

A lover of Tarot, moonlit nights, and the enduring promise of a new dawn, Vixen strives to prove that love —in all its forms—is the universe's most potent magic.